DIAMANTAIRE

DIAMANTAIRE

THARA TLAU

PARTRIDGE
A Penguin Random House Company

To order additional copies of this book, contact
Partridge India
000 800 10062 62
orders.india@partridgepublishing.com

www.partridgepublishing.com/india

to city of the sun

ACKNOWLEDGEMENTS

So many thanks to those whose support I always treasure: my dad, who left for his heavenly home midway of the writing of this book; Eunice; my family and relatives; and close friends. Special thanks to my valuable sources out there whose names I can't mention here. *TOI* Surat edition is of tremendous help in writing the book, for its regular coverage on the diamond business in the city. I extracted good resources from Asiatic Library, Mumbai, and Kavi Narmad Central Library, Surat. I'm really thankful.

The sin of Judah is written with a pen of iron, and with the point of a diamond: it is graven upon the table of their heart, and upon the horns of your altars.

The book of Jeremiah 17:1

PROLOGUE
Surat, India

Bartolomeu Dias reached Cabo das Tormentas in the southern tip of Africa in 1488 in search of a *spice route* to India that would circumvent the Muslim-dominated North Africa and West Asia. Ten years later, Vasco da Gama circumnavigated the Cabo and reached South India. The Portuguese were the first in medieval Europe to establish business interest in India, trading mostly in spices, the *hottest* medieval commodities. Their successes drew the attention of the English, the Dutch, and the French to India, who later on established their own trade concerns and factories in different port cities.

The English set up their first factory in India at Surat in 1613 by obtaining a firman from Emperor Jahangir and slowly consolidated their business and political influences in other parts of India from here on. In the midst of the arrivals of strong European traders in India with the backing of their respective governments, the eighteenth century saw the silent and uneventful arrival of a lesser-known but distinctly vibrant trading community in the port city of Surat—the Jews.

The first Jews who migrated to Surat were of Iraqi-Mesopotamian origin and hence the name Baghdadi Jews. They first arrived at Surat in the early 1700s; steadily consolidating their presence for permanency, they established a synagogue in 1730 and a dedicated Jewish cemetery soon after. They were educated and talented craftsmen; they practised a flourishing trade dealing in diamonds, silk, indigo, opium, jewels, and other important trades of the time, forming an enviably strong trading community. They were undeniably one of the potent harbingers of flourishing European trade in western India, proficiently playing the role of middlemen and mending trade links between the Europeans and the local traders.

Among the most successful business families of the Baghdadi Jewish community were the Tobis. Hosea Tobi was inherently an influential businessman, dealing efficiently with the vagaries of the different trading communities of the time. He was equally in the good books of the Europeans and the local traders, sustaining his business interests within stiff competition between the Europeans and the local trading communities without any foul play undermining the interests of either side. This made him inextricably the most sought-after business partner indispensable to both trading sides. After his death, his son Jedidiah Tobi took over the reign of the business with almost equal zeal and capability, but with much stronger fervour and grace.

After Jedidiah and by the time of his next descendant's departure from the scene, there was no such family left behind to be identified as the direct descendants of the first Baghdadi Jewish settlers except the threadbare lineage of the Tobi family; they had migrated out to different cities in India and abroad. Two centuries after their arrival, even the first census of Bombay State (the erstwhile state of Gujarat and Maharashtra) of free India in 1951 mentioned just a minuscule presence of the Jewish community in the state and that too predominantly of the Bene-Israelites principally residing in the Greater Bombay (city) area of the state. The Baghdadi Jews didn't find any mention in particular.

In 1960, the states of Maharashtra and Gujarat were born out of Bombay State due to linguistics-based state reorganization in India. The succeeding year of 1961 was the decadal general-census year in the country. The census data of 1961 showed a meagre presence of only 515 people in Gujarat who claimed to be Jewish in origin and dominantly residing in Ahmedabad City area. The city of Surat, where the Baghdadi Jews established their first permanent settlement in India, became significantly devoid of the population, at least on record; the Jewish cemetery in Surat, with epitaphs carved on the tombstones in calligraphic Hebrew, became just remnants of the past, symbolically reminiscing Jews' deaths centuries ago. Probably, the only remaining family of the Baghdadi Jews might be too insignificant a number to occupy the dotted lines of the census data to justify the Jews' presence in Surat. To many, the crumbling tombstones in the Jewish cemetery at Katargam in Surat were just artefacts artfully portraying the Jews that were once present in the city but were now supposedly extinct.

But to the Kathiawadi Gujaratis dealing in diamonds, the Jews were still very much there, though forgotten by the world; the only remaining family still wielded strong enough clout as if *omniscient* in the diamond business.

CHAPTER 1

In the family genealogy, the eighth down the line of descendants of Hosea Tobi was Ezekiel Tobi. He married a Desai of Navsari, Bhumika Desai, from whence the sheen of Jewish blood was *contaminated* for the first time in the family lineage. What brought Ezekiel Tobi to the Adajan locality of Surat across the Tapi River from the bustling old neighbourhood of Katargam was evidently not circumstantial but bestowed with intrigues, unbelievable to most and suspicious to some. He was the scion of a Jewish trading family whose diamond cutting and polishing business was very successful till then when his mother Hannah was alive and at the helm of the family business.

Though his father died when Ezekiel was just a teen, at eighteen, his mother boldly accepted the responsibility of running the family business, unrelentingly ignoring the dominant position of men in the diamond industry. She had partly learned the art and perhaps the intricacies of the industry from her father-in-law and, later on, her husband.

Though she basically was not from a business clan (daughter of a Paradesi Jewish rabbi of Cochin Synagogue down south), she had the temperament needed to intimidate and outclass fellow diamantaires in bidding and selling rough diamonds and polished goods.

She had exponentially and so controversially done wonders to the family business, turning it into the fifth largest polishing house in Surat, which might not have been a likely scenario even had Ezekiel's father been still alive. To depict the enormity of her business acumen, the Kathiawadis trading in diamonds referred to her popularly as Daughter of Tapi after the mighty river slithering through the city, the second largest river of western India revered as a goddess by Hindus. Her influences were touted to be running deep across Hoveniersstraat, the legendary diamond quarter of Antwerp, to the by-lanes of Johannesburg's CBD. One diamantaire in desperation had even cropped up a theory on the existence of a *Jewish triangular cartel*, an underground alliance of the world's leading Jewish diamond businessmen, pointing fingers at the dominant families of the Finkelsteins in Antwerp, the Oppenheimers of the De Beers in Johannesburg, and the Tobis of Surat.

Another interesting but rather deceptive rumour which found many acceptances across the diamond trading communities of Surat was that she had been receiving abundant supply of roughs via Dubai from the diamond barons in Tel Aviv who had good access to the Russian mines largely owned by state-run Alrosa, which were almost absolutely inaccessible to the Surti diamantaires and were comparatively better-priced than Africa's. This was also believed from the fact that the diamond barons of Tel Aviv were not happy with the growing clout of Surat's cutting and polishing industry, which had dried up their dominance in the Far East and Hong Kong markets, and so a Jewish family in Surat was being patronized to counter the growing dominance of the Kathiawadis in the diamond trade.

This rumour grew louder with wider anticipation when Hannah spurned an offer from a celebrated rough-diamond importer for a partnership to tap the potential of importing ores from the Marange mines in Zimbabwe despite Kimberley Process censure and international sanctions. It's an open secret in Surat diamond market that without a trifling exposure to illegal ores, the business is too cruel to survive the market damnation with the ever-fluctuating demand and price. Many a times the price of polished goods plummets down to worth even less than the original purchase price of the roughs. But you have to dispose of the goods. Stockpiling finished-diamond inventories for a long duration was not a norm here, and blocking liquidity inflows was too risky an affair. You better do round-tripping, reimporting the goods you have exported, taking advantage of the laxity in taxation law, and benefitting imperatively in income tax payments as well.

'If she couldn't source illegal ores from Russian mines, indulgence in blood diamond is a matter of survival, not a matter of ethical extravaganza,' quipped the celebrated importer.

Whichever contours might the constant allegations take shape to, Hannah stood steadfastly unfazed, too ambitious to immerse herself in mundane frivolities. Her business remained largely unperturbed and was doing extremely well. Hers was a business ran with prudent and insightful acumen and blessed by the indulgence of an unseen hand behind—*liaison*.

Unfortunately, things could not be rosy forever in the household of the Tobis in tandem with the business achievements. Hannah, a rubicund woman who cherished good life and good food and who had a history of astoundingly healthy forebears, showed an alarming decline in her health and body though she was only in her early fifties. This was unheard of in the history of her paternal family, who boasted of good appetite for food and sex even till their late sixties, displaying their machismo in splendour. Her deteriorating health caused her anxiety mentally, causing stress with the fear of losing grip on her mental stability to run the business and family affairs.

'My bones are wilting,' she would say when asked about her problem. 'And that's the root cause of the on-and-off fever and tingling sensation in my body.'

On any attempt to let her be examined by physicians, she would have pretexts or endless reasons to avoid the move—like missing dearly her late husband; family practice of self-healing meditation; no consultation of doctors unless suffering from proven terminal illnesses; or market fluctuation causing her anxiety and fear. She was always steadfastly adamant on her *belief*, and no request could convince her to change her stand. This was until she was bedridden, with constant high fever, joint pain, and regular diarrhoea. Only her bones were not wilting; in fact, her body was wilting away with untreated pneumonia, which had been plaguing her for so long.

The physician who saw her was flummoxed. 'She has consumed herself to death with her stupidity,' he said.

As the physician said, her body had long been consumed by the pneumonia, and it was futile an attempt trying to decelerate the degenerative process. After a week of fervent pursuits, the physician suggested, 'She can't be cured any more except by miracles. But we can keep her away from the pain and suffering until her last breath.'

Hannah died of pneumonia and of her stupidity. Her body was laid flat on a mat in the middle of the living room and covered with a white dupatta. People gathered and waited for words from the son. The son muttered a few words, and the body was carried by a hastily arranged hearse towards the bank of Tapi River. She was not accorded the Jewish traditional dead-body grooming of *rechitzah*, *taharah*, and *halbashah* nor the simple recital of the liturgical burial prayer, Kaddish, but she was offered the chanting of the Vedic text by the local Hindu priest. She was cremated, and her ashes were gathered in an earthen pot, following the local tradition. The *besna* ceremony of the Hindus was held on the fourth day after her death. This was the first time that besna was held for a death in the Tobi household, a far-flung departure from the conservative Jewish tradition.

Hardly two weeks after Hannah's death, Ezekiel, his wife, and their two children left for Adajan on the other side of Tapi, selling off all the family's interests in business to arch rivals, barring just the ownership of the main building that had once housed the cutting and polishing business, which too was now rented out to a once-rival outfit. The main suspect of the move was the last words of Hannah before her death, though there was no way to confirm it but hearsay.

CHAPTER 2

Ezekiel Tobi had well adopted 'Gujaratiness' with fond veneration since his early teenage days. Not only did he fall in love with a local girl, whom he married later on, he openly celebrated the Gujarati way of life, indulging in the festivities of the local people, most enthusiastically the Navaratri. Very regularly, he danced the garba in full vigour during the whole nine nights at a stretch ever since he first stepped into high school. His mother dictated to him to settle down with a Jewish girl from Poona, whom she met once at a Jewish gathering in Bombay's Knesset Eliyahu. He took Bhumika home, faking her to be two months pregnant. That was all that was required to convince his mother to arrange for his marriage with Bhumika Desai of Navsari in a month's time.

But the marriage approval came with a rider. The prescient Hannah made Ezekiel swear a promise that he and his wife would go to Cochin to study the Torah and the essence of Judaism under his grandfather's guidance for a period of one full year.

Initially, this 'sabbatical' period could not produce much dent on Ezekiel's already strong attachment to Hinduism; he was least interested in a religious culture originating from somewhere in the eastern Mediterranean region when he could profess the virtue in the religion of his birthplace. But later on, he accidentally discovered a new passion during the sabbatical—a study of Hebrew literature. He came to admire the Torah as a great work of ancient Hebrew literature, and it was his main focus of study during the one-year stay. He confessed that had he not developed fondness for Hebrew literature and admiration for the exquisite literary qualities of the Torah and, more broadly, the Tanakh, his one-year sabbatical would be the most torturous year of his life. His interest in the Torah as a great work of literature had a lasting impression on him till the later days of his life.

Hannah believed in the Star of David, Ezekiel believed in the Saptarishi. She observed Sabbath by keeping it *holy*; he observed Guruvar by fasting till sunset. Notwithstanding their religious differences, such a contrasting mother-and-son duo made up the best of business partners. She was the face of the family business to the outside world, dealing with customers and diamond traders, while he was the darling of the workers. Since his teenage days, he took obsessive interest in the welfare of their diamond polishers, which made him very popular among them. He maintained good industrial relations with the workers even without any knowledge on what were written about in PR or HR books, which the HR professionals themselves might not be too eager to comply with. The extraordinarily popular initiative he undertook when he was just twenty-one to prevent his workers from being poached by other polishing houses made the town flutter with admiration and disgust alike.

He conceived a system of *ownership sharing*, which was yet unknown in the diamond industry then. It was not like the now-quite-popular employee stock option plan of allotting stocks to the employees or any other complicated way of preferential share allotment schemes but a 'tenurity' scheme where 50 per cent of the net profit of the organization was shared directly among the employees, depending on their service longevity in the organization. A service of six months was the minimum requirement to earn benefits from the scheme. Six months to one year of service earned ten points, after which a year-on-year addition of ten points went on till five years of service. Twenty points are added to an employee's benefits after the completion of five years of service and above. So the point score decided how much an employee would receive from the fifty per cent of net profit being shared to the employees. This benefit was over and above an employee's regular salary, which too was in par with the industry standard of the time.

The scheme was not only instrumental in withholding skilled workers from jumping over to rival cutting and polishing houses but also in encouraging workers' participation in running the business to achieve a larger and more wholesome profit margin for a share of bigger and fatter slices of the pie. Every worker knew that the lesser the number of workers, the bigger his share was. So even when there was a dearth of workers in the industry, their workers tried to fill the vacuum very enthusiastically, engaging themselves more with a sense of ownership of the business and belongingness indeed. This introduced a good sense of discipline in the workforce, ensuring that they run their own work schedule without much interference from the family. Ezekiel's inborn HR skills and Hannah Tobi's *liaison* together catapulted them among the families in the top rung of the diamond business in no time.

No doubt, Ezekiel had a very deep sense of respect for his mother's merchandising skill—in acquiring and selling diamonds in the local and international markets—but not without a slew of scepticisms and a tinge of prejudice at how they could fetch much higher profit margins than their peers in the industry, the highly professional ones included. The one thing which caught his curiosity more was the abundance of roughs, rough diamonds, for them at any time of the year even if it was declared a lean season for others.

His curiosity grew even more so post the outbreak of the allegation by a rival diamantaire of the existence of the unholy nexus, Jewish triangular cartel. He had often heard his mother murmuring 'Liaison' in her business dealings but couldn't brave to confront her with his suspicions, fearing her being dismayed.

She had once confided confidently, 'Son, unless *liaison* fades away, nothing would deter our business growth. Believe it.'

He had reluctantly convinced himself to believe the words of his mother and preferred to assume rather than confirm that *liaison* was a term in business lingo that meant 'partnership' or something close to that, not a secretive implement rarely applied in the diamond trade.

She had called him up on her dying bed, requesting all others to leave the room. She spoke, 'Ezekiel, my son, my time to depart will come soon, and I will be leaving behind a thriving business which you and I have so passionately built together from the midpoint where your father have left it. You have proved yourself a good businessman in building good rapport with our employees, one of the three cornerstones of our success. The second cornerstone is the market, both for sourcing and dispensing, which is partly in our hands and partly in Jehovah's. The third one is *liaison*, which I have acquired by sheer providence and which has become our shield and guide throughout this auspicious journey. As a last wish of your mother, I request you to follow the trail of *liaison* and discover the source, my godfather, to convey my special thanks to him personally since I could not do so in my lifetime.

'When your father died, I received a letter after a month or two from a man in Nairobi, Kenya, who signed it off with just the initials JT. He said I could be a part of the liaison if I wished to continue your father's business. He asked me to meet a man named Irfan Rangoonwala from Dadar in Bombay, who was already a member of *liaison* and would take care of our requirements of roughs unlike your father's, which depended heavily on local auctions. He said Mr Rangoonwala owed him his life, so he was highly indebted to repay him back in any form and service. If I wanted the service of *liaison*, he would make sure I would receive regular flow of roughs via Mr Rangoonwala at a price at least 40 per cent lower than the prevailing international market price. But this should be made strictly to the limit of 70 per cent of our overall business requirements so as not to provoke unnecessary suspicion from other local diamantaires. It meant we still need to source 30 per cent or more of our requirements from local auctions and international markets.

'I decided to give it a try . . . to verify the authenticity of the said liaison. I did have a premonition that the meeting was going to be a game changer for our family business. I went to Bombay and met Mr Rangoonwala to forge a partnership, as suggested by Mr JT, with bliss in my heart and the perception that our days of high growth was coming forth with the back-door support of a strong godfather, like how so many of our fellow diamantaires have the backing of dons from the Bombay underworld. The details spelled out to me by Mr Rangoonwala were not just alluring but truly devoid of any mischief and all for the good of our business. There was not a speck of hidden agenda in the conditions just to push through one's business interest at the expense of others. Everything was amazingly awesome and acceptable at one instant . . . except for one clause.'

CHAPTER 3

It was during the reign of General Ne Win that a large exodus of Indians from Burma happened. General Ne Win, who seized power through a military coup in 1962, was prolifically xenophobic. Despite his Chinese ancestry, he persecuted ethnic Chinese and ordered a large-scale expulsion of foreigners largely of Chinese and Indian origins. His policy of wholesale nationalization of private enterprises alone was responsible for the forced emigration of more than 300,000 Indians from Burma.

Many of the uprooted Burmese Indians returned to India via the land border, penetrating to Assam. Many halted to settle there, while many proceeded to mainland India, preferring their ancestral lands scattered across different regions of India as their destinations. Among the emigrated lot were very few Muslims who could trace their origins in Rander near Surat. And among the emigrated Muslims with roots in Rander was the father of Irfan Rangoonwala.

Irfan Rangoonwala's grandfather Ismail was a successful trader and a highly respected Indian community leader in Rangoon. Not only were his successes beneficial to his family, but he also contributed a large chunk of his wealth to the educational and health causes of Burma. His contribution towards the establishment of Mandalay University (previously Mandalay College) was among the largest in terms of money—largest indeed if counted in proportion to the riches of each contributor. His hefty donation to upgrade and improve surgery in Rangoon General Hospital was hailed as the second most important event after the establishment of the hospital. The most important one happened much later after Ismail's contribution and decades after his death. It was the speech delivered at the hospital premises by the pro-democracy fighter Aung San Suu Kyi, her first public speech after her return to Burma, a landmark development in the annals of democratic movement in Burma.

By the time Irfan Rangoonwala's father, Abdul, started charting the waters alone after the death of Ismail, General Ne Win overthrew the Burmese government by a coup d'état. The general's forces were most uncaring towards those people whom they termed resident aliens, among which many and in a large majority had long ties with Burma. They were largely the second- and third-generation Burmese Indians, born and brought up in Burma, who had innate fondness towards Buddhist pagodas as much as their own places of worship and who instinctively smeared their cheeks with *thanaka* daily during the long summer months.

Abdul and his wife were forced to flee Burma by the junta. Their harrowing days as refugees crossing the land border and encountering the greatly insufficient as well as inefficient caretakers arranged by the government of the Republic of India were like daylight nightmares haunting them the rest of their lives. He and his wife survived the treacherous journey to reach Rander near Surat with one of the most limited rations provided to refugees in history.

Abdul started off as a roadside vendor to support his family—him and his wife. Luck was by his side. His Burmese delicacies were an instant hit among the Randeris and spread wide to Surat City as well. He slowly consolidated his livelihood and, two years later, launched a new business venture—which many people that time thought was risky and not profitable—mainly from the proceeds of the sale of his family's wealth of gold and diamond jewellery, which they had smuggled out from Burma, and his few savings in Indian rupee. He was even mocked by a close friend who predicted his reversal to roadside business again soon.

That was when he started off with a textile business, dealing exclusively with *resham* (silk). Silk printing was not a big thing among the textile businessmen at that time and unlikely to be profitable in the near future too. This was the opinion of veterans with more than three generations of operation in the textile business, not amateurs. However, Abdul dared to put his fortune and risk his second life, his life after deliverance from the Burmese military junta, into starting a business on resham printing for export to other cities and even abroad in the future, as he could foresee a brighter prospect much ahead of others.

The year was 1964, and that was when he saw the birth of his first son, who was christened Irfan Rangoonwala. The business was prospering faster than anyone in the know of textile business could speculate it to be. That was the time when fashion in Bombay was catching up with what was hot in the European fashion streets. His resham business expanded fivefold even just three years after its launch. He was like a patron saint to those who followed his footpath later on and went gung ho in adopting resham business.

By the time of his second son's birth in 1968, he was already a true mogul among the Surti textile traders. His opinions were respected far and wide and resonated at every corner of Surat's vast textile markets. Under his initiative, a cartel was formed to outperform other silk exporters, mainly from South India, in the Asian and European markets. Before this cartelization, every businessman was a unit fighting alone for his own survival and suffering from his own debacles in times of crisis. Under this cartelization, all the silk-trading businessmen were working together as a single unit for the common good and, in the process, cutting down output expenses and thinning down risks of loss due to external factors.

After the formation of the cartel, the dominion of silk export shifted from South India to Surat in no time.

When the going seemed strong and stable and emerged firmer each passing moon, the story of the family's success suffered a heavy jolt from within and very unexpectedly when the older of the sons, Irfan Rangoonwala, decided to go against the family's newfound success and start a new venture of his own and that too at a very relatively young age of twenty-four. He was supposed to take over the family business from his ailing father in a few years. His stream of choice too was not making things easier to absorb by his parents either.

He wanted to start a diamond jewellery export firm with diamond cutting and polishing units as affiliates and that too in another city, away from his parental comfort zone in Surat, Bombay. His father would initially fund the venture, Irfan propounded. And he would repay him back in instalments, if demanded, after achieving the break-even point, which he calculated would be attained in about six years' time. He would entirely surrender his rights over the family's textile business to his younger brother and would never lay claim to his family's properties in the future.

It's an abdication of one's responsibility towards his family. Abdul grieved silently for days at the decision of his heir apparent trying to figure it out what exactly had prompted him to do so. *The family needs Irfan more and more and will depend on him more and more in the coming days due to my faltering capability,* he lamented within.

Though apprehensive, Abdul finally decided to accept Irfan's challenge, taking it in his stride. 'In business, we have been blessed since our fathers, turning anything we touch to gold. Rangoon has given us the opportunity once. Surat for now, and Bombay seems to be the next frontier,' he exclaimed ostentatiously, clearing the air of any worries he might secretly be nurturing.

CHAPTER 4

Quite unusual in the diamond business, Mr Rangoonwala's business address was located at Dadar West, Bombay. Diamond trading and its allied activities were mostly confined in and around Opera House of Charni Road. Moreover, the address didn't evince close semblance to that of a seasoned diamond trader's; it sounded rather awkward, more like a typical neighbourhood jewellery shop.

Mrs Hannah Tobi tracked down the address of Rangoonwala & Rangoonwala Jewels without much effort nevertheless; not so far away from the railway station, it was prominently located and surprisingly very well known in the locality. Contrary to her expectations and intuitive belief, the address was of a jewellery showroom, a handsomely designed high-end shop with exquisite exhibition of designer jewellery on the display windows. She had anticipated Irfan Rangoonwala to be an exclusive stone dealer like her but with a much wider interest in import and export.

The showroom was an independently built entity, ostentatiously designed, a bit aloof, and distinct from those congested shops in the vicinity sharing common walls for want of space in the cramped gali. It had two captivating Roman columns standing tall and grand, sandwiching the main entrance dominatingly like the two strong and reliable arms of a father holding the torso of a child on her first lesson in walking. It was a two-storey building, but from the outside view, the building appeared like a tall single-storey structure due to the imposing tall independent pillars and the huge display windows on both sides of the door.

Mrs Hannah Tobi was greeted warmly at the entrance and welcomed to the showroom by a maharaja bearing a long moustache.

'I'm here to meet Mr Irfan Rangoonwala,' said Hannah to one of the ever-smiling female attendants inside.

The attendant enquired if she had an appointment.

Hannah shrugged. 'I don't have any formal appointment as such, and I didn't know that it's required. Anyway, if you can pass on a message to him that a certain lady by name of Hannah Tobi has come to meet him, I will be thankful,' she replied.

'I will do that. Please be seated there. I'll be right back,' the attendant said politely, pointing her left index finger at an empty chair positioned nearby, and left for the upper floor through the gold-plated stairway.

Mr Irfan Rangoonwala appeared at the corridor on the upper floor before long, displaying a doubtful look mired with optimism. He took a tentative step forward and then carefully strode down the stairway, with his eyes aimed at Hannah with unmistakable warmth. The employees of the showroom were perplexed in seeing their boss coming out of his chamber to meet a visitor; it was quite unusual for the man. This might be the first time he had done so, if they could recollect correctly.

'Mrs Hannah Tobi, I'm so pleased you came. My *liaison* has been worried by your late turn-up. I thought of coming to Surat to meet you had you not turn up this week,' said Mr Rangoonwala in a voice sounding with concern and grace.

She responded with a visible tone of appreciation in her voice, 'I'm thankful for your warm gesture, Mr Rangoonwala. Things were not as usual after my husband's death, so I could not turn up earlier.'

'Let's move up to my cabin and continue the discussion there,' Mr Rangoonwala said, leading Hannah towards the stairway.

'I hope you will appreciate knowing how *liaison* works,' Irfan Rangoonwala started as they entered the cabin.

'Hopefully so . . . if you can convince this old lady,' Hannah said with a light-hearted smile.

'This liaison works purely on trust. Nothing else. And this is not for a year or two. It's for the lifetime of the partner and not more or lesser than that. You can't let your child inherit the privilege of being in the liaison. If you die, it ends.'

'In this relationship, there will not be more than three members. Now, you are the third member as wished by Mr JT, who seeks your well-being as his highest priority,' he continued.

'Who is this Mr JT, by the way, to have so much concern for me from faraway Nairobi, if you don't mind revealing his identity?' she quizzed him.

Irfan looked at Hannah assuredly, his expression empathetic, and said, 'It's not the most important thing for you, and me perhaps, to know and understand him in depth. I too hadn't met him personally before he rescued me from the threat of the underworld don Mahmud, though I already had business dealings with him for years. I benefited from his generosity numerously after that episode—yes, numerously, but I met him again for the second time only due to his concern for you and your family's well-being.'

Hannah didn't make further demand, obliging Irfan dutifully as if paying obeisance to the glory of the Ten Commandments of Moses to the Israelites.

Irfan spelled out the provisions and the unwritten clauses of the liaison to Hannah without any hesitation of mentioning in between the lines the dark days he had swam across with the help of *liaison*.

'There is no looking back,' he concluded proudly.

At the end of the session (yes, unlike a deal-making business meeting with mutual discussion and persuasion, the meeting appeared more like a session on your visit to the dentist, with the dentist lecturing you on the benefits of maintaining oral hygiene and you behoved to being just a mute listener), Hannah Tobi could shed almost all the hesitations she had harboured in becoming part of the alliance. It appeared that every aspect of the relationship was in her favour and was going to work for the good of her business. So . . . she would join.

But the only hindrance was the unwritten 'no heredity' clause, perplexing her with the thought of the future of her only child fearing for the worst while sustaining the business in such a competitive environment with no godfathers to support him in the event of her death.

Let the future decide its own course, she convinced herself half-heartedly, and she agreed to join the alliance.

CHAPTER 5

There was a sombre display of calmness in the room like the calmness displayed by loyal soldiers in laying wreaths on the grave of a brave commander who had died leading them in the battlefront. The atmosphere was more of melancholy than helplessness. Like the soldiers still possessed by the valour of their departed commander, there was a distinct peculiarity in the room from the presence of a strong force, a dominant one. It was not emanating from the artistic frames and souvenirs or the beautiful tapestries hanging on the walls, but a sense of its presence was being felt by the five senses of the body.

As Irfan Rangoonwala entered for the first time the residence of his *liaison*, he found himself being hypnotized by the presence of the force. He could feel that it was the dwelling place of a man of high honour. Though Irfan had corresponded several times with the man who had been the saviour of his business when he was on the verge of extinction, he hadn't had the slightest chance to meet him in person again at his house nor anywhere else, not even to shower him with his gratitude after he salvaged him from the death gallows, from the hands of the dreaded killer don.

Today, he was invited to begin a new assignment, a responsibility which Mr JT would not love to see fail. Irfan knew he owed his loyalty, his blood, and his whole family to this man and whatever responsibility was thrust on him would be obediently carried forward. Irfan also knew that throughout their engagement as *liaisons*, Mr JT had never demanded any outright favour from him in return though he had benefited enormously from his generosity. He was slightly nervous at being summoned for an assignment since he knew quite well as a person living in Bombay what the underworld don meant by 'assignment' when he summoned his 'pointsman' for the job.

Security guards had let him a free passage and guided him from the gate till the doorway of the house without frisking him or causing any hindrance, which itself made Irfan more curious and uneasy. As he walked into the hallway and entered the living room, his mind wandered around inquisitively as if bewildered by an unseen force.

In a few minutes, he was greeted from behind by a tall black gentleman who seemed to have known him for so long.

'Mr Rangoonwala, we are pleased to have you here,' the black man said politely.

Irfan turned back and responded, 'I'm happy too to be invited here to meet Mr JT.'

The black man surveyed him briefly from his forehead to his neck and said, 'You look rather tense, Mr Rangoonwala. Maybe distant travel has taken its toll. Please be seated there on the sofa and relax for a while. Mr JT will be here in five minutes.' The black gentleman pointed at one of the immaculately designed seats adorned with giraffe skins and well positioned at the corners of the room. Then he left.

Mr JT entered the room from the back door. 'Mr Rangoonwala, we have been looking forward to have you as our esteemed guest here. How is your mother-in-law doing now?' he said while entering.

Mr Rangoonwala found himself off guard at the remark. *How did Mr JT know my mother-in-law in Ahmedabad fractured her leg? He seems to be tapping on my every move. Whether for good or bad, only God knows.*

'Ah . . . she's doing fine now, sir. And I'm pleased and feel privileged to be invited here to be your guest.'

Mr JT shrugged and asked him to accompany him upstairs to the terrace above the living room. The terrace had a good view of the vast expanse of the plain towards the wildlife game reserve on the western fringe. Mr JT had carefully chosen the setting of his residence, his estate, on the outskirts of the city, within the realm of the exquisite beauty of the wildlife sanctuary, and away from the bustling neighbourhood of Nairobi.

Mr JT said, 'Mr Rangoonwala, I've been backing you up all these years and been helpful to you when you needed me the most.' His throaty voice was as commanding as the sound of the strumming of a bass guitar in a music orchestra.

Irfan just nodded his approval without saying a word, but he felt that he was going to be tasked with some kind of favour or possibly Mr JT was going to make some rightful demands from him this time.

'I've not asked from you any favour except for the smooth sailing of our business by being *liaisons* to each other throughout these years. And I'm not a kind of person who will do that unnecessarily and have never done so in my whole business life,' he continued.

This made Irfan more inexpressive, with a feeling of being made subservient to his benefactor.

'But things go outside the realm of my influence where I need to protect my family lineage and the inherited business.' The words of Mr JT sounded apologetic now but determined, which made Mr Rangoonwala wonder if he had become a person competent enough to protect Mr JT's family or if he was going to be used as a pawn for the purpose.

'I'm at your service, Mr JT. You have been my godfather and protector throughout these years without making any unreasonable demand for favours in return even though my business's survival is largely in your hands,' said Irfan submissively. 'It may be that your family or lineage, as you said so, is in real trouble since you have called for my attention this time after being business contacts for many years and in *liaison* for about three years now without any face-to-face meeting.' The expression on his face displayed his seriousness on the job ahead and the importance which Mr JT might have attached to it.

'My progenitors, let me tell you, were from Surat,' Mr JT said graciously.

Irfan pulled up his brows in amazement, wondering at how this man from Nairobi—who was more whitish than brownish, who did not possess the facial structure to be of Indian descent but more likely of central Asian or Eastern European descent, and who had not even spoken a word of Hindi in their long years of association—could make such a claim, but he pulled back his reservation, giving space for Mr JT to continue his narration.

'I'm one of the descendants of the first Jewish settlers there. Our family lineage had gone down with only one son and with one or two daughters, with the only son taking over the father's trade, till my brother and I arrived at the scene. It was the first time in the family history since my ancestors arrived in India that two boys were born in the family. There was happiness as well as confusion looming large in the family over how the inheritance of the family business would go on from there. I first learned about the confusion when I was about twenty-two years old when I overheard my father and grandfather discussing about splitting the family business into two.' With a pause, he looked at Irfan Rangoonwala as if expecting his reaction on the revelation of his family's ancestry.

Irfan sighed and said, 'Splitting a family-run business can be problematic at times aside from the emotional impact it carries,' trying to give the impression that he understood what Mr JT intended to say.

Mr JT shook his head and continued, 'Yes, that was what I too felt even at that young age. So I tried to confront my father on their decision and also to tell him what I had in mind after a prolonged thinking after I overheard the discussion between him and my grandpa. One day, I found a chance to confront my father all alone when he was in their bedroom. I asked him about his plan, and he said the business had to be split equally for the brothers and for the sake of the family. I displayed my strong disapproval and told him the business we were running was not that big and splitting it further would deteriorate the chances of survival in a very competitive market.

'I told my father that since I was the elder of the brothers, I would start my own business venture outside India with his blessing. Our ancestors had landed in Surat armed only with their whims and skills, but they successfully carved out a niche in the merchant business, competing with the strong Europeans and the local traders. My father protested and said those were the days when adventure had paid rich dividends but not any more. "You can't live with your fancy, comparing what was true then and what is true now," he told me decisively. However, my father knew how stubborn and determined I could be. So instead of simply obstructing my decision, he asked me to lay out to him my proposal for my future business as soon as possible.'

Irfan Rangoonwala interrupted, 'My family too had lots of reservations when I decided to go beyond the comfortable zone of our family's textile business, which they found was safe and where our intuition lay.'

Mr JT nodded at Irfan Rangoonwala's interruption approvingly and continued, 'And I told him I was going to South Africa in search of fortune. I didn't know how the name South Africa sprang up in my mind that time. It was a clear voice of destiny that spoke on my behalf. To cut it short, five years later, I left for South Africa with a few thousand rupees in my possession. My brother inherited the business, branching it out to retailing finished diamonds in the local market. I was very happy when he married a beautiful Jewish girl from Cochin. That was about nineteen to twenty years back, and later on, they had a son. However, I was deeply pained and shocked by his untimely death at the age of forty-seven due to malarial fever about two weeks ago. Now, protecting his wife and son—our family's only lineage—and their business interests for their survival is thrust upon me, as my father too had died a few years after I left for South Africa.'

Irfan asked suggestively, 'So you think I can play a role in it?'

Mr JT replied, 'It just means that a third member, and probably the last partner, would be admitted in the liaison. Her business will be protected and supported courtesy of you. And I'll always play the role of your protector and supporter on the other side by being your loyal *liaison*.'

'Agreed!' said Irfan enthusiastically, raising his voice a pitch higher. 'Tell me the plan, and I will follow it. Deal.'

Mr JT spread out to Mr Rangoonwala the details of the interlinkages between the members of *liaison*—since another member would be added—and the new business flowchart, which in all likelihood seemed to have more affinity to *the preamble of the constitution* of a banana republic or, more contextually, the text of an oath of secrecy of a secret society than the charter of partnership of twentieth-century business partners.

After all, it was faith in the members, as it had always been, that would command the success of the partnership more than the norms and the by-laws. They both knew trust would prevail over all unintended errors committed and omitted in the days to come. This trust had been built subsequently from the day of Irfan Rangoonwala's rescue from the clutches of death and the consequential birth of their brotherhood. And this trust was irreversible between them; even if a new member was added, it would be the mainstay of their liaison in the coming days.

CHAPTER 6

Irfan Rangoonwala was a successful diamond jewellery exporter to South East Asia. His successes had drawn him close to the political establishments of the leftists and the rightists and even the centre-rightists, ebulliently rolling out funds for their political campaigns and, to some individual political heavyweights, for their *pockets*. He lavishly gave discounts on purchases of diamond-studded jewellery by wives and mistresses of political bigwigs and top bureaucrats at a price even unpolished diamonds and raw gold wouldn't fetch and sometimes even much lower than that and to the privileged ones, the influential few, as gifts for 'unknown' gratitude.

His establishment had never experienced an income tax raid. He could proudly hold up and display a record as probably being the sole business establishment in Bombay City with such a magnitude of trading but not ever being raided by the Income Tax Department, an exceptionally preferential treatment. However, he was once visited by

Directorate of Revenue Intelligence (DRI) officials for purportedly paying less custom duties and undervaluing his gold and diamond imports. He made an impromptu visit to South Block in New Delhi, which houses the Finance Ministry, and that was all that was required to keep the DRI at bay.

The business and the political clout all went well until the great Tom Yum Goong crisis appeared in the scene and started ravaging the South East Asian economy mercilessly. The Singapore market was on tenterhooks, the Malaysian economy showed great signs of stress, the Thai economy was in quandary, and the Indonesian market was astonishingly bearish. Consequently, the purchasing power of the South East Asian people dwindled down unbelievably, in some places, reaching the point of arson in the streets for food and life-saving drugs. There was a complete halt on the import of lifestyle items and, to some extent, drugs and agricultural produce—not by the governments but by exporters from other parts of the globe due to the shattering creditworthiness of the countries.

With no payments coming forth from his exports to the South East Asian countries and with little chance of the economy to recover from the bruises within a year or two, Irfan Rangoonwala had a big chance of going bankrupt. Bankruptcy would bury not only his business but also the lives of his family, he was sure. His assets would soon be confiscated by the bank on loan recovery if he could not arrange for payments for another few months. Then what would be left for his creditors who were lending him unsecured loans, the people from whom he regularly procured raw gold and rough diamonds in credit mostly from the underground market, with payments being given only after receiving proceeds from sales abroad—basically, the South East Asian market?

He knew the bank did not pose enough of a threat to him and his family physically, though it could legally confiscate the assets he had pledged against his business loans. It was the gun-toting dons of the Bombay underworld, who were undeniably funded by the international diamond barons, that were ruining his family's safety. The dons, he knew with certainty, would strike hard where it hurt the most, which would apparently cause insurmountable bereavement, if not repentance, for the rest of his life—if his life was ever spared.

That foresight of fear and impending danger soon intensified when he received an unusual visitor at his office in his plush jewellery showroom at Dadar one Thursday afternoon. The man who came was well known for another type of business dealing—*supari*. *Supari* is a term used in Mumbai underworld for contract killing. It was a dreaded term, obnoxious to the establishment, and people who have made their names in supari contracts have a stranglehold in businesses varying from real estate to the movie industry. Dealing with this man would be an unusual experience for Irfan Rangoonwala. His presence in the room itself displayed an aura of sadness.

The man was in his late forties, or possibly early fifties. He looked sombre and serious with an unruly tobacco-stained beard, manifesting a no-nonsense businessman character. His name was Salim Ahmed but was revered in the underworld business corridors as Mahmud after the infamous Afghan invader Mahmud of Ghazni, who plundered western India mercilessly in the eleventh century AD. He had been accused in nine murder cases, including the murder of a popular Hindi movie playback singer. However, he had been convicted in none of those cases due to the lack of 'reliable' evidence.

'Irfan, this is a high time you pay back the money' was his opening line.

Irfan Rangoonwala did not want to appear confused or perturbed by asking which one of his many underground creditors Mahmud was representing.

'The South East Asian market is boiling now, and chances are that it will recover in a year or two if goodwill prevails. I will pay back the money then with all the interests accrued in line with prevailing moneylending rates,' Irfan Rangoonwala replied.

Mahmud said with a tone of condescension, 'We are not dealing with the South East Asian market. It's you we are dealing with. Don't dare to hold up our money that long. Otherwise, be prepared to face the consequences.' He rose up from the seat to leave.

When the dons themselves visit their 'targets', it is always a case delivering extreme compulsion with most likelihood of an attack in the near future if warnings are not heeded. It's a sign requiring immediate attention, for building up self-protection options or lining up remedial measures for real war. Negotiation at this time is seldom acceptable; only the physical delivery of the demand is appreciated. So hard-cash payment had to be arranged to deter any possible attack on the business or the family, which could otherwise inflict collateral damage with bleak chances of recovery ever again.

His residence, a spacious upmarket apartment at Lower Parel, had been mortgaged. So what was left of Irfan was his jewellery showroom with the entire inventory of platinum, gold, silver, and precious and semi-precious stones and diamonds. Even a sell-off of the entire inventory along with the showroom itself would fetch him just enough money to pay back his underground creditors and the bank somehow. That itself was an end with not much future prospects for his family to rebound back to normal life. At least they'd retain their apartment to live in rather than ending up in one of the gigantic slums in Bombay suburbs akin to the notorious favelas of Rio.

Attempting to employ the goodwill he had garnered over the years with political bigwigs would be impractical here since no politician with his pie in the electoral process of the estranged democracy would dare to entwine himself where there was involvement of shady dealings and, most apparently, the stakes of underworld dons. Political bosses were useful only when there was involvement of public authorities, like the police, the IT Department, or the intelligence agencies. Should he otherwise sum up all his courage and face the underworld don so that even death would be with a kind of dignity other than being summarily bankrupted and continuing to live life with self-hatred and ending up a laughingstock for others?

Incidentally, amid all these chaos and coercion, he had another high-profile visitor at his office after two days of Mahmud's call. This time, it's from a rough-diamond supplier from Kenya, a non-producing country but with great deal of influence among Mumbai's diamantaires and underground players alike. His initial, JT, was as authoritative in the underground market as the initial KP for Kimberley Process for the segregation of diamonds in the international market.

'Mr Rangoonwala, I have heard about your payments being held up in the South East Asian market turmoil,' he said.

Irfan Rangoonwala said, 'That's why now I'm not only on the verge of bankruptcy but sacrificing the safety and lives of my family as well. And I know you are also here today to roll out your rightful demand for early payment.'

JT replied thoughtfully, 'So far, I have not done business by despising my partners and patrons when they needed help the most. I've stood firm by them even at the expense of losing my prestige. Today, I came all the way from Nairobi not to make my rightful demand as you blemished me to be but to lend you support, to stand by you, and to put you back on track to your rightful place.'

These words of comfort from Mr JT were rather shocking than surprising, least unexpected in the prevailing scenario. Irfan was like a comatose patient with the unlikelihood of recovery blinking his eyes as if to compose his vision in a vegetative state. Or could he be more like a death-sentenced criminal whose clemency was announced when the noose of the hangman's knob was already looped around his neck?

This might be the most soothing verse Irfan Rangoonwala had ever heard in his entire life; truthfully, even the first confession of love by his wife was not more soothing to his ears than what he heard today from Mr JT.

The consequent conversation was warm and cordial and resonated a brotherhood intimacy in the tone. It coalesced around the threat perceptions, the credibility involved, slightly on the volatility of the South East Asian market, and the threat of Mahmud, who seemed to represent some of Irfan Rangoonwala's creditors, including JT—until his visit today.

'I will take care of the threat from Mahmud and the shortage in the supply chain. Henceforth, you will not be my buyer alone, you will be my *liaison*, and the same applies to me too. It is a brotherhood based on trust,' JT concluded.

This was a baptism of faith, the laying of the foundation stone for the business alliance to come to shape, and this would influence the culture of diamond trading in future. And for Irfan Rangoonwala, it was more like the arrival of the happy ending scene of a skilfully crafted tragicomic drama.

After JT left Irfan Rangoonwala's office, he called up his hitman in Mumbai to his hotel room to discuss about the Mahmud episode and the way to handle it. The hitman was dreaded in Mumbai for his expertise in silent execution of targets unlike Mahmud, who was famous for his hit-and-run method, even using assault rifles like AK-47 openly to spray bullets at targets. His hunting style in the notorious Mumbai supari market had earned him the epithet Black Panther, which appeared quite phenomenal not only for his unblemished dark-coloured skin but also for his style of hunting so quintessentially feline. He was also well known for his stringent approach to acceptance of contracts no matter how much money was involved or offered.

His decision was always based on the purpose behind the contract and whether the man to target really deserved the 'death penalty'. To carry out an execution just for the sake of prize money was not his style of doing business. The man supposed to be targeted should carry enough weight of sins and condemnations for death. He abhorred offers from businessmen and politicians just to settle old scores or for personal vendetta without enough evidence of misdeed by the target to qualify for the death penalty.

The man in question was Vincent D'Souza of Goan heredity and a hesitant Catholic by birth, not by choice. His entry into the underworld order and his rise in rank and popularity were also not of his choice but the outcome of sheer necessity coupled by capacity. He was one of the main accused in Harshad Mehta's stock scam, which rocked the Indian stock market in 1992, the largest and most widespread security scam ever recorded in Indian history. He was a small-time stockbroker but with close dealings with heavyweights like Harshad Mehta and some other high-profile persons involved in the scam. His life was at risk, and his arrest was imminent after the suicide of the chairman of a nationalized bank, with the uproar demanding for the heads of those allegedly involved in the scam becoming louder, and the story hitting news headlines even more sensationally as public outrage boiled up.

The scam had made him move underground unwittingly for sheer survival, and that became the turning point in his life, converting him from a stockbroker to a supari broker. His past experience in the brokerage and securities market and his vast dealing experience with businessmen of all hues were unmatched even by those people already tenured in the underworld business, mostly the offshoots of labourers in the slum dwellings. Within no time, he was the head of an underworld *family* with disciplined members unlike other underworld families, whose spontaneity in hooliganism earned them hatred and scorn from the public and law enforcers and even from the slum dwellers, who were the mainstay of their activities and safety.

His family became the most sought-after protector of business interests spanning from diamond trading to real estate developing and from stock trading to supari broking (supari broking for those who wanted to observe top secrecy and maintain blatant obscurity with the most unlikelihood of their names coming out publicly even if things went extremely awry against the plan). The supari broking, especially, did come not only with hefty fees but also with high selectiveness in acceptance. Vincent D'Souza did not simply accept contracts, particularly those involving the murder of people, if he was not fully convinced of the 'ethicality' of the purpose.

Vincent D'Souza was well known for his style of leadership, a leader who led from the front. Any assignment involving killing a target was planned and pursued by him, himself leading a selected few who were well versed in the art of 'clean' murder, murder without leaving any suspect evidence behind. They had never been traced for any of their murders for lack of credible evidence, though highly suspected in some of the cases. In one case, the investigation even almost zeroed in on them.

It was the killing of a gutkha (chewing tobacco) tycoon who was autocratically controlling the gutkha business in western India and whose love for 'good' sex had enslaved, spoilt, and also killed so many gullible young models hunting for space in Mumbai's filmdom and fashion world. He disdained any sign of competition in his domain and wilfully silenced anyone who dared to challenge him in his field of business. This had earned him the wrath of small businessmen who dutifully, out of fear, had to bow down to his dictate.

When the secret conglomeration of these small businessmen approached Vincent D'Souza for the supari contract to kill him, he blithely accepted the contract without the slightest hesitation.

'He is the man I've wanted to bury underneath for so long. It's not only for the way he runs his business empire, silencing his business competitors mercilessly, but look at the number of innocent young girls he has trapped, spoilt, and even killed! Even if you have not approached me, just another confession from an enslaved girl would have compelled me to send him directly to hell,' he spat out his hatred for the gutkha tycoon as his acceptance speech for the contract.

However, the killing almost went kaput with the tripping of his finest henchman on the second floor of the gutkha tycoon's three-storey mansion after the action. A brief gunfight with the guards of the house ensued, resulting in a greatly difficult exit for the team, four of them in all, from the scene. The man was severely injured in the left leg, and this compelled them to go to a hospital far enough from the tycoon's residence in south Mumbai.

The henchman had to be compulsorily hospitalized for the severity of the injury. But hospitalization of the man was a death trap for them. Since the life of his family member was of utmost importance always to Vincent, he decided to admit him in a hospital as the plan B for escape taking over at the apparent failure of plan A.

He told him, 'In any interrogation by doctors and police, tell them you had a bike accident near Borivali National Park at the crossroad on the way to the railway station. The registration number of your bike is MMX 1845, a black Rajdoot.'

They left him alone in the hospital. His supposed 'cousins' arrived soon after, as per plan B, to take charge.

At around 1.45 a.m., not even an hour after the henchman was admitted, a police jeep arrived at the hospital, one among the various teams dispersed in Mumbai City to look out for the injured killer in the city's clinics and hospitals since the guards at the mansion reported that one of the assailants had been injured falling down from the second floor of the house.

The doctor and nurses on duty at the emergency ward of the hospital confirmed having a man with severe left-leg injury due to a bike accident, who had been brought in by some passersby. The police team headed to the bed where the henchman was lying, groaning nervously with pain.

The inspector patted him on his shoulder and conducted a brief interrogation. The henchman sounded innocent and ignorant of the purpose of the interrogation, being a professional whose pay cheque depended on his ability to avoid police network. He was steadfast on his standpoint and was adamant that he had forcefully hit a bump due to his speed under poor street lighting and was thrown out of the bike on the road, while his bike hit the elevated pavement and tumbled up on the side.

'It's unfortunate,' he said repentantly.

Though the police inspector could not recollect conclusively, he could vaguely remember that he had seen the photo of a man who looked so similar to this man in a dossier containing the activities of Vincent D'Souza when he was posted at Crime Branch a year ago. When the inspector asked him if he knew of the don Vincent D'Souza, the henchman replied politely that as everyone in Mumbai did, he too knew the don, whom everyone feared and respected.

Unconvinced, the inspector and his team proceeded towards the crossroad where the henchman said he had met the accident. There they found the bike as described by the man, bearing the number plate exactly as had been narrated. The accident seemed sufficient enough to cause the fractures the man had suffered; the bike had flown off the pavement after hitting an abnormally protruding and badly highlighted speed breaker. The henchman was exonerated.

JT said, 'I want this Mahmud to stop meddling with Irfan Rangoonwala's business. He should be warned about it.'

'Mahmud is not a type of person who will listen to anyone once he is bought for a job. Nothing can stop him,' Vincent D'Souza replied.

'Then how will we make him stop interfering? Can he be that stubborn to death?' asked JT.

Vincent D'Souza replied, 'He would prefer to die than play second fiddle to us or anyone in the underworld supari market. And he has crossed the line with me several times, for which I have given him enough warnings. I'm not going to warn him again but kill him. Even in Irfan Rangoonwala's case, he can blow a strike any time. He is the kind of person who wants to earn a name from fear and terror. In most cases, when he shows himself to his target for a warning, he already has a timeframe in hand and a potential point to strike to inflict heavy damage.'

'Then he must die. We can't brook any infringement on our legacy. Let his clients also know that Irfan Rangoonwala is under our protection and we don't appreciate business with unfair intimidation,' said JT.

CHAPTER 7

Mahmud is a Friday regular at Star Trek Bar and Pub at Colaba, the most popular weekend destination in Mumbai. The owner of the pub, Ramesh Patil, is his protectee and a regular subscriber to his fund-raising programmes. Mahmud has received three high-end supari contracts from Ramesh, who was among Mahmud's very few close confidants. He felt at home there and most often landed up there without any bodyguard accompanying him.

It was pertinent that Ramesh Patil should be made a witness if Mahmud was to be killed so as to effortlessly spread the news with terror to Mahmud's other clients. It would also be prudent of Ramesh not to report to the police the perpetrators of the crime; as an eyewitness, he would be risking the future prospects of his business. He should be mum about the incident even if interrogated rather than play with the sentiment of the now-ruling underworld don, Vincent D'Souza.

Ramesh Patil makes it a routine and an obligation to be always present at the bar on weekends, particularly on Friday nights, since it was on these nights when most of his fashionable clientele, the crème de la crème, and illustrious names in Mumbai City would want to set foot in his bar. On the upper floor on the southern end facing the seafront were four cubicles aesthetically designed and rented only to customers of the highest social standing and status, like presidential suites in ultra-luxury hotels. The one at the left corner was permanently reserved for Mahmud on Friday nights. If he didn't turn up, it would be empty for the night, but he seldom let it happen.

Since Ramesh Patil was to be made a witness to the killing of Mahmud, he had to be involved in the scheme of things but pragmatically only in a supporting role or most probably as a lead actor. His close friend, their family doctor, was dispatched as a messenger, as none from Vincent D'Souza's family would be permitted, in no uncertain terms, entry into the high-walled compound of the residence even to just relay a message.

Ramesh gave the highest priority to the security of his home, and he was a family man who delved himself soulfully into anything concerning family members or the family nitty-gritty. His visitors were only his well-known acquaintances; otherwise, they are the taxmen. Forced entry into Ramesh Patil's house could spoil the plan and trigger an unwarranted underworld battle from which a bloodbath between Mahmud's family and Vincent D'Souza's could ensue. The doctor relayed the message to Ramesh Patil verbatim and also handed over an envelope containing the dos and don'ts in the unfolding of events and, audaciously, the photos of places where bombs were planted at his daughter's residence in Pune, which could be triggered off at any time if Ramesh didn't comply.

Ramesh was tasked with two simple jobs. Number one and the most crucial, he was to lace an excess of methamphetamine in the alcohol served to Mahmud on the Friday night when he was all by himself and without any other soul in the bar or anywhere else knowing about it. This was a very dangerous cocktail for those with heart ailments; Mahmud had a history of two bouts of severe heart attacks in the recent past. Number two, when Mahmud collapses with an attack, Ramesh should dial the emergency ambulance number provided by the municipality, which had been tapped by Vincent D'Souza's men. If a call list was sought in any event of unmitigated police investigation, this would dilute any possible suspicion.

The Friday night saw the trickling in of regulars, the highs and the not so highs, and some new faces looking apparently awkward and cloyed by the superfluousness of the interiors and the robustness of the bouncers, who were unbelievably polite and friendly—and overfriendly to the female gender. Mahmud's partner tonight looked high voltage and top end. She was a blonde, presumably Russian or Caucasian in origin, with a voluptuous body frame, a facial feature bearing a strong squarish jaw, and a matching feathered-weave hairdo. The duo moved up unhindered and carefree to the upper floor and into the cubicle well laid out and specially reserved for Mahmud, with a personal waiter greeting them at the entrance.

The couple was served, a bottle of scotch for Mahmud and a bottle of beer for the lady, along with Mahmud's favourite savoury plate—steamed crab legs with drawn butter and lemon wedges and a plate of non-spicy mutton *seekh* kebab.

A little over half an hour later, a vividly wild scream—a howling one, in fact—broke out from the cubicle at the left corner. That was the cubicle being occupied by Mahmud and his partner tonight. The waiter ran in and saw Mahmud lying on the floor, curling on his left side with his knees tucked in, and the lady in despair, sobbing beside him. Other people came rushing towards the cubicle, and along came the owner, Ramesh Patil, who was, even days before, precariously all too aware of the doom that was going to happen. The lady explained with shock and stammerings filling her lips how Mahmud complained of a sudden pain in his left chest and, a moment later, collapsed on the floor. Ramesh Patil immediately ran back to the bar counter and dialled the emergency ambulance number provided by the municipal corporation in a list of emergency numbers for fire, police, etc. and particularly suggested in Vincent D'Souza's letter.

The ambulance arrived at the spot in about twenty minutes. The bulky body was hurriedly moved into the van, the stretcher hoisted shakily by two lean and seemingly underpaid attendants. The ambulance sped back, sounding the sirens, towards the hospital without any emergency procedure being performed on the spot. Ironically, the ambulances of this particular south Mumbai hospital were ill-equipped—a paramedic and two helpers following, with a humble first-aid kit for attending road accidents and some construction-related accidents prone to the area, not for a cardiovascular kind of emergency that would require oxygen cylinders and other complicated medical equipment to salvage the heart patient in the most critical hour.

The ambulance manoeuvred through the narrow streets adjoining the bar on to the main road approaching Regal Cinema. Just before reaching the turn at Regal Cinema, the van suddenly careened around violently left and right. The driver applied the brake steadily, and the van screeched to a slow halt. The driver got down from his seat and momentarily saw the tyre below the driver seat completely flattened. The puncture almost seemed to him like a case of sabotage because the tyres were recently replaced with brand-new ones and with new tubes too about a week ago. However, he soon reconciled himself in thinking, who on earth would be so cruel as to touch a life-saving vehicle?

He rushed to the left bank of the road towards a public telephone booth and dialled up the hospital emergency number to rush another ambulance in a hurry. Another crucial thirty minutes was lost in the process. By the time the ambulance reached the hospital, the body was literally soulless. Mahmud was rushed to the emergency operation theatre, and desperate attempts by doctors and nurses to resuscitate him followed, but all were in vain—too little too late probably. He was declared 'dead on arrival'. The bartender who had accompanied Mahmud in the ambulance identified him as Salim Ahmed, the dreadful Mahmud of Bombay underworld.

The nearest police station was informed immediately of the incident; the victim brought in supposedly of a heart attack turned out to be an 'almost' outlawed fugitive— 'almost' only by the political patronage he had been enjoying. Mahmud had never been convicted of felony or any big crime. Though he had been accused of murder and attempted murder and grand larceny, his charges had always been diluted by the Criminal Investigation Department of the police, or CID in short, which was controlled by the home department, and he always walked out a free man.

A police team arrived at the hospital in a mad rush and flung themselves across the corridors frenziedly, like the decimation of concentrically arranged black and white coins by the striker at the start of a carrom game. A quick examination of the dead body was done to confirm if it was really the dreaded underworld don Mahmud. It was confirmed after a quickie comparison with police records about Mahmud's identity. The information was relayed to the city deputy commissioner of police (crime), who ordered to arrange for an autopsy the night itself. A forensic physician from Cooper Hospital, a police surgeon, was apprised of the situation and told to be ready for an emergency post-mortem with his team of medics; meanwhile, the body was carried towards Vile Parle, where Cooper Hospital was situated.

Briefly, the autopsy result confirmed the cause of the death as heart attack. The external examination did not find any sign of harm or wound.

'The likely cause of the sudden heart attack is drugs,' commented the forensic physician. This could be ascertained only by further invasive investigation and examination requiring extensive medical testing. He recommended preservation of the viscera for further investigation.

Honestly, the police were exuberant with triumph at the death of Mahmud, a criminal so elusive and too well connected to apprehend. However, as a matter of policy and policing, the cause of the death was to be investigated since there was a likelihood of drug-induced death and could be a case of murder; the murder angle was also a likely scenario since Mahmud had no proven record of drug use, though he was a casual drinker. If it had not been for the adverse comment of the forensic physician, the police would have liked to close the chapter at the hospital itself. Still, they were against the preservation of the viscera for further investigation in the event of suspicion of foul play. They wanted the body to be disposed of from the face of Mumbai City and humanity itself as soon as possible.

The body was sent for a silent burial at a distant forest near Khandala only after two days of the incident. The body was buried by wrapping it with only a white loincloth so that the body would decompose faster. They didn't want to give a chance to any further cumbersome investigation to prove his cause of death even if any other court case springs up later. Let the body decompose faster so as to deter any further investigation. Let the body decompose incognito along with the soil, the soil he had bathed several times with blood of his fellow human beings, and let the remaining be only a lump of mud.

A sub-inspector with two constables arrived at Star Trek Bar and Pub the next afternoon to assess the circumstances leading to the death of Mahmud. From the rank of the head of the team and its members, it was perceptible the investigation was a casual formality and not a serious one— just to close the case with propriety to avoid a possible legal tangle in future. The team questioned Ramesh Patil and a few of the employees as to how Mahmud arrived at the pub, his behaviour, how he was allotted the special cubicle, and lastly, why an emergency number was dialled instead of hurriedly proceeding to the nearest hospital with a taxi in such an emergency situation. For all these, Ramesh Patil had a ready-made and well-tailored textbook answer.

'Mahmud arrived rather sombre that night, accompanied by a blonde Western girl. The sombreness was not typical of

Mahmud—possibly due to indulgence in some kind of drugs before they headed to our pub,' he replied.

As for the allocation of the cubicle, he said anyone in the pub business who didn't want to see his shop ransacked one fine morning would always surrender to the demands of a man like Mahmud, who is cruel, egoistic, and had a capacity to create terror. 'No bar in Mumbai worth its salt is free from such visits, as the police department is well aware of,' he added exultantly.

The phone call part was indeed tricky, and so he was apprehensive, but the most intrepid part of the murder plot was in the critical hour after the heart attack, letting the effect of the drug become more invasive and accumulative. And so that was why this part was skilfully planned by Vincent D'Souza to deceive any suspicion in an event of a police investigation.

Patil convincingly said, 'We are supplied with emergency numbers by the municipality for any kind of eventuality— fire, riots, and such incidents like this, which requires emergency medical attention. We follow the guidelines stringently. If not, we are being stared at our doors by a possible close-down. Businesses such as bars and pubs are most susceptible to possible close-downs for not following government guidelines. Should I dare to risk my business by taking a half-dead body to a hospital by a taxi? I wouldn't do that. I would rather dial for the emergency ambulance number and wait for the response whatever may be the outcome.'

The police were outwitted in this case. Or the police were not interested to pursue further a case they were not too eager to prolong. The death of an underworld don, whatever the cause, was rather a cause for exhilaration for them.

The case was closed, and so was the chapter of Mahmud's exigencies in Mumbai City. Ramesh Patil could have been entrapped for further investigation had the police opted for further examination of the body or viscera of Mahmud. Vincent D'Souza had mixed what was supposedly methamphetamine in a dose of 60:40 proportion with arsenic powder; the perfect poison—tasteless and odourless. He had wanted the mixture, the poison, as invasive as possible. He couldn't risk failure in this particular attempt; the repercussions were too ominous and disastrous.

Had there been no heart attack due to the methamphetamine effect, the arsenic poison would still be tantamount to a fatal reaction sooner; he had this as a forethought. Moreover, Vincent was instinctively right in his calculation that the police would not want furtherance of the case involving the death of a high-handed murderer like Mahmud, who was so elusive and so well connected politically to be captured. His death—and that too, not in their hands—was a cause for extreme jubilation for them. If it had been in their hands or in an on-site encounter, the top-notch officers of the police department would have suffered the heat from the political front.

The death of Mahmud stirred out mixed responses from the business fraternity of Mumbai—from the underworld supari contractors to the upmarket lifestyle managers. To many, it was a moment for jubilation. But to those few who treasured their association with the don, the situation was gloomy and pale, like the moment the losing team embraced the sound of the last whistle to end the final match in the FIFA World Cup. With their shadowy protector decimated, the followers of Mahmud succumbed to hibernation in a flurry, and his business protectees fumbled about to fend for themselves in any eventuality.

The message to the creditors of Irfan Rangoonwala was loud and clear as intended and had more pragmatic effects than expected. No debt collector arrived again in his office, and instead, one creditor, who was well endowed with a large real estate business and rough-diamond import, even came out with a flexible piecemeal offer for repayment of the debt as and when the South East Asian market rebounded and with another line of credit if required.

This act of kindness by JT, which was precisely not a simple deed of affection but a profound act of salvation, not only emancipated Irfan Rangoonwala from the grip of extinction. He had been in the death gallows, facing the wrath of his creditors, who were severely ruthless in recovering their debts in any way, like bloodthirsty vampires wooing for blood in the death of nights. It also humbled him enough to understand the virtues of human beings, which he lacked badly till then, being the least concerned for his subordinates and the poor. His attitude towards life tilted towards the positive, and he started believing in the dignity of man, whether beggars or billionaires. On top of this, he pledged his life, his blood, and his service to his unheralded saviour, to whom he owed abundantly.

CHAPTER 8

JT was the initials of Jonathan Tobi. As a teenager, JT was flamboyant and nefariously (un)popular in the neighbourhood for his benevolent attitude towards the fairer sex and with a tinge of youthful debaucheries to his credit. He skilfully penetrated the hearts of the local lasses, his smooth texture of golden hair and shades of Burmese sapphire-looking eyes giving him an upper hand among his chums.

This was true to the writer of the book of Qoheleth in the Jewish's Tanakh, who said:

וכל אשר שאלו עיני לא אצלתי מהם לא מנעתי את לבי מכל שמחה כי לבי
שמח מכל עמלי וזה היה חלקי מכל עמלי:

> (I denied myself nothing my eyes desired;
> I refused my heart no pleasure. My heart
> took delight in all my work, and this was
> the reward for all my labour.)

He could trustfully depend on his star every time he fell for a girl—save for one—howsoever conservative she might have been gossiped to be. There were rumours doing the rounds among his contemporaries of him being impotent, for the girls he had allegedly laid hands on had never been pregnant. Later, he might have exhausted all his luck, or bad karma might have prevailed, when he chose to go after a girl seven years younger than him and who belonged to a family with political might. The girl didn't understand his advances through awkward gestures and accidental bumping, but her father did. The father threatened to outcaste JT and his family from the society if he saw him venturing even just within 100 feet of his daughter whenever, wherever.

His archetypal hard-working nature and dedication at home had earned JT the confidence and goodwill of his father to lead a lavish, and also a devilish, life outside at the expense of those girls who fell for his beauty and wit. His sudden departure from the scene at the age of very late twenties, a ripe age to marry (though rather late for the local boys but still appropriate for the Jews), had caused enough ripples of suspicions from being driven out by the father of his latest crush to the wildest assumption of him turning into a sannyasi, renouncing his earthly sins and moving to the foothills of the Himalayas.

JT demanded of his father, 'Dad, it's been four years since I last presented my proposal to move out of town, most probably out of India, to establish myself and my own interest in business. I've been your faithful lieutenant those four years, as you undoubtedly know. Now, it's your turn to shower me with your gratitude.'

His father, with his usual repertoire of wisdom, replied, 'If you are really that determined to leave the house of our ancestors, who am I to force you to quit your intention? This shows the Jewish blood in you is still pure and running high with the willingness to conquer a new angle of entrepreneurship. Our forefathers, who first descended here in Surat from Mesopotamia, were not forced out from there due to hardships or hatred of the community. They were here to quench their thirst of exploring newer avenues for business, leaving behind the fertile valleys of the Euphrates and Tigris, which were fertile not only for agriculture but also for business, being the melting point of oriental and Western commerce. Every Jew who moves out of his ancestral home to make a mark for himself never brings blemish to himself, his family, or the community. If you can carry on that tradition, you have everything you want that this house can afford.'

JT was surprised by the straightforwardly affirmative response he received from his father. He had prepared himself for a struggle if the situation demanded, to fight for his right to determine his own future. His father had never shown any leniency in letting him off in those few years till he poured out his demand today. It was a pleasant surprise, an unexpected one.

He said with elation in his heart, 'I'm as determined as my forefathers were to bring laurels to you, my father, to my family, to my community, and to myself. And I will be at your and my family's disposal any time under any circumstances if any need arises. As for my request for your help, I think my travel expenses to reach South Africa and enough money for a month's survival are all I need.'

His father, in a serious note, replied with trepidation, 'My son, for a man armed with so much determination, only a wonderful future beckons, I can acknowledge. But mind this, you are going to a country where racial segregation is in practice . . . very rampantly. This means trouble is brewing hot, and a revolution of great magnitude is possible any time. Animals can be oppressed and suppressed, but the spirit within an oppressed man can never be suppressed. That's what makes a man distinct from an animal. You stay away from any form of discrimination against your fellow human beings if you want your fortune to be intact.'

JT nodded approvingly and wondered deep in his heart how his father could always fill his words of advice with an aroma of wisdom. He felt he was going to miss it badly when he was far away from him and also realized that he was already missing it.

His father added more words of caution, 'Never take a decision when you are worried. Never hasten to reply when you are angry. Never make promises when you are very happy. As for the money, I will give you double of what you have requested for. You are going to a strange land, and a strange land can spring up surprises in strange ways—good or bad. You will need it if unexpectedly the bad happens, but hopefully not.'

He cautioned JT that his plan of moving out of town and his destination should be only within the family. 'Let no other soul know about it,' the father quipped.

CHAPTER 9

JT had heard that Johannesburg was called I'Goli in Zulu, which means 'city of gold'. *What does the City of Gold have in store for me?* he was thinking while waiting for his turn to catch a taxi outside Jan Smuts International Airport.

He settled for a men's budget hostel called Witwatersrand Backpacker Lodge, which was about thirty to forty minutes' drive westward from the airport, not only for the dirt-cheap daily rent and the good connectivity or proximity to Braamfontein and Central Business District but also for its ideal location, strategically speaking, near the city suburb of Yeoville, which was dominated by Jewish immigrants. He self-convincingly believed that by virtue of him being of Jewish descent, he could seek first-hand help from the people there at any instant of untoward racial skirmish, which according to his father was brewing hot due to the prevailing apartheid regime. He knew he wouldn't be there for long since he reached Johannesburg not as a blind fortune-seeker but with the knowledge of what he wanted to do and how he was going to proceed. He needed a place to settle temporarily just for a few days—at most, a fortnight.

Witwatersrand Backpacker Lodge was a popular destination for budget backpackers and cash-strapped jobseekers reaching Johannesburg mostly from different parts of South Africa. Its location at Hillbrow offered an *almost* quality life at an affordable range for an indecisive stay. For backpackers, Hillbrow was an ideal location with its numerous not-so-trendy pubs and bars, street markets, theatres, and the risky but entertaining nightlife, with easy twenty-four-hour transportation to different parts of the city. For jobseekers, proximity to Rosebank and the city centre was the biggest factor for deciding to put up at Hillbrow and at the most affordable lodge—the Witwatersrand Backpacker Lodge.

JT had been in contact with a social worker of Dutch origin by the name of Johann van der Watt, who was based in Johannesburg and whom he had met twice while on trips to Bombay. He had promised him the riches of the Dark Continent if he could move down to Joburg to assist him.

The first meeting was accidental; the second, coincidental.

The first one was when JT accompanied his father on a trip to Bombay for a business dealing with their long-time trusted family friend Mukesh Jain at the hurly-burly of Opera House, the diamond district of Bombay. Mukesh had introduced Johann van der Watt, who was there with him, 'He is the *citadel* of native diamond mining and controls the shadowy trade from discreetly mined diamonds from Southern Africa. And most of all, he's a great social worker, taking care of the street-stalking homeless children. Without his supply, the diamantaires in Bombay would have lost out due to the monopolistic attitude of the De Beers, which control almost all the legal diamond trade in South Africa and the neighbouring countries.'

This frank introduction by Mukesh without any inhibition at revealing his true identity had made Johann van der Watt confident and comfortable about the father–son duo as people whom he could put his bets on. They were the typical diamond-trading Indian family whom he could trust, as Mukesh Jain trusted them immensely by telling them without any hesitation about his business and personal activities in one go.

From their first meeting, JT had developed an instant liking for the man who could abundantly control the other side of the diamond trade, the shadowy part, and soon dragged him into an eloquent conversation about his work, the risks involved, and the chances of his participation, if he so desired to taste the risks. Till then, Johann van der Watt had never sensed such keenness from any of his business friends in India about diamond mining and the highly dangerous trade-off involved and, that too, from a person who seemed so juvenile in the trade.

He had told him metaphorically, 'It's worth the pinch. If you are a person who can gauge challenges with action, come and join me.'

These words of Johann never escaped JT's mind thereafter. He had longed to chance upon another meeting again with the lord of the illegal diamond trade. He had rued the fact that he had not confirmed then his determination to participate in the trade and aid Johann.

The second meeting was purely coincidental and extremely significant for both JT and Johann and, later on, for *liaison*. Johann van der Watt came to Bombay to attend a seminar at Bombay University as one of the keynote speakers on Child Labour in Third-World Countries as a part of the South–South Dialogue process between countries of the southern hemisphere. JT also came to attend the seminar as a part of the college delegates among the largely drawn college students from western Maharashtra and southern Gujarat to create awareness and to draw the attention of college students to the negative implications of child labour in the society.

Johann van der Watt was the *unproclaimed* star speaker at the seminar. The participants were impressed and deeply moved by the knowledge and service of the star-footballer-turned-*messiah* of the vagabonds. His work in adopting and rehabilitating orphaned street children and his dedication to their future well-being and education served as a good example to the participants and as a reminder to the other speakers of the need for grass-roots level of participation and accumulation of practical knowledge in fighting the social evil.

His experience was unparalleled, he seemed quite authoritative even among the expert speakers, and his knowledge of the subject was full of practical applications. He was the only speaker who displayed practical knowledge of the negative social impact of uncontrolled child labour and exploitation. The rescue mission he undertook about five years before, which almost cost him his life, was what earned him the friendship and respect of many South African anti-apartheid fighters, including his lifelong friend Raymond Zulu. The revelation of this story was what kept the participants and speakers in rapt attention, herding them into one faith, one baptism.

There was a boy named George whose father was an alcoholic but was the sole breadwinner of the family. The father worked in a textile factory in the suburb of

Johannesburg City; it was owned and run by an only-white management company. This textile company was one among the very few which provided retirement and accidental-death benefits to the employees by way of deducting every month from the salaries of the workers a small amount of money as insurance premiums. Every worker's life was insured under a group policy of the company. However, the company always demanded a replacement if an employee died and the family of the deceased claimed the benefit. Only when a person from the family enrolled as a replacement would the company release the insurance amount.

George's father was not only an alcoholic, but he was also a member of a street gang which patrolled the streets of the suburb at night for toll collection from hawkers and street vendors. He worked in the factory in the afternoon shift and roamed the streets with the gang members at night. The control of the toll collection was under constant dispute between two rival gangs in the area. There was great misunderstanding in their area of supremacy, and a fight for absorbing more areas under their dominion was a regular occurrence. In one of these gang wars, George's father was fatally shot at his temple.

When George's mother went to the office of the company to claim her husband's insurance benefit, she was, as was customary in all cases, rebutted with the unwritten rule in the company about the replacement of the deceased worker before the release of the insurance amount to the family. She was a mother of two children—George, twelve, and his sister, eight. She couldn't leave her children at the mercy of her notorious neighbourhood to enrol herself as a worker in the company, and George was still too young to take up a job. When George's mother pleaded for mercy, stating her difficult situation, the company bosses rebuffed her with a single statement, 'We are not running a charity home here.' They, however, revised their condition this way after her incessant pleading—she would be at home, but the boy George would be enrolled as a ward boy.

Johann van der Watt heard about the plight of this poor family from the mother of a boy in his rehab. He went on to meet the management of the factory to negotiate for the peaceful release of the boy from forced labour. The negotiation ended in Johann being thrown out of the factory premises and handed over to the police on charges of interfering in the functioning of a public company and disrupting the peaceful atmosphere of the factory.

Johann was released on the second day of his judicial remand on furnishing a bail bond. He took eight men to the factory that very afternoon to secure a forced release of the boy. They could have thwarted the boy from going to the factory, but they wanted to perform a symbolically dramatic release of the boy from the factory to show their disagreement and abhorrence of the inhuman and anti-social practices of the company. They made forced entry into the factory premises and directly proceeded towards the section where the boy was engaged in. They pulled out the boy from his workplace and marched towards the gate from where they had forced their entry.

That was when the top manager of the factory arrived at the scene followed by a few armed guards. Johann and his men were commanded to halt their movement immediately. Without paying any attention to the shouting, Johann and his men, along with their rescued boy, proceeded stubbornly towards the gate to make their exit from the premises. The manager ordered his men to fire at the intruders. The guards fired about three rounds of bullets at Johann and his men. Johann was the unfortunate one; a bullet hit his left shoulder.

The gunfire brought all the factory workers rushing out of their work floor towards the scene. On seeing Johann bleeding and the other men being manhandled, the mob of workers in rage stormed at the guards and the manager. Some groups of workers in the meantime ransacked the factory premises indiscriminately without showing any sign of pity and reluctance. Johann was immediately rushed to a nearby hospital by his friends. No life was lost, but the melee ended in a great setback for the company with the huge loss on damages to the factory premises. A commission was set up by the government to investigate the alleged inhuman practices of the company.

JT was amazed and also surprised more than others at how destiny could bring them together again, the chance he had been fantasizing for so long and yearning for so badly.

'If I've not been destined to be a diamond smuggler, this type of rare coincidence would not have happened,' he whispered to himself. He could only appreciate how Johann could effortlessly toggle between social work and smuggling—two differently poled activities that were so varied in purpose and so contradicting in style.

The opportune chit-chat on the sideline of the seminar was how JT was anointed to be a diamond mercenary and how Johann was convinced that Jonathan Tobi would prove to be a good partner in smuggling.

Anointing JT to be a fortune hunter in Africa, Johann said, 'If your Jewish blood conditioned by Indian mercantilism is anything to go by, you are going to make it big in the trade. You have both the adventurous Jewish trait and the finest trading trait of Indian merchants imbibed in your blood. The treasure hunt is in your favour.'

This was perhaps a great turning point, an upheaval indeed, in the life of JT. Then a new life was born in him, a revolutionary one.

CHAPTER 10

Johann van der Watt was a professional football player before he decided to move down south to Johannesburg. He had played for several clubs, including the great PSV, before he shifted back to his hometown, Rotterdam, to play for the local club Feyenoord, the club Rotterdam was well known for. He was a member of the UEFA Cup winning squad in 1974 and was one of the most probable players from among the highly hopeful, deserving, and promising Dutch players from the big clubs of Netherlands to represent the country in 1976 World Cup finals if qualified. His name appeared in the list of eleven players which the newspaper *Algemeen Dagblad* proclaimed as the dream team for Netherlands in 1976 World Cup, though he would have been thirty-two by then.

He was in his prime, enjoying his popularity and his good earnings from his contract with the local club, when he decided to quit professional football one fine Good Friday morning in 1975. He appeared at the city's landmark St

Laurenskerk Church and waved at the sports journalists who had been trailing him due to the speculation of him leaving Feyenoord for AFC Ajax. Words had done rounds that Johann van der Watt would make a decision on Good Friday. AFC Ajax had been offering him an intrinsically handsome contract, the second largest contract money in the history of Dutch football, but on Good Friday, Johann announced his retirement from professional football unexpectedly but exuberantly. This surprised not only the journalists—who immediately went berserk, volleying loads of questions, comfortable and the not-so-comfortable ones, at the retiring footballer—but also equally his family members who were with him that time but were as ignorant as the journalists of his surprising decision.

He quit professional football unceremoniously and flew down to South Africa like a Christian missionary in the eighteenth century sailing down to the dreaded Dark Continent to spread the *gospel*, denouncing the pleasure of being part of a civilized society and the riches of the industrialized world. He made Melville, a Bohemian suburb of Johannesburg, his home. He founded a rehabilitation home for children of black labourers and dedicatedly worked for their welfare. His earnings in Dutch gulden as a professional footballer were large enough to support about thirty children his rehab could hold for about eight good years, he calculated. There was one thing he didn't foresee in his calculation—one day, his fortune would dwarf his earnings during his entire footballing years, semi-pro and pro days counted.

It so happened that one day, Emmanuel, the father of a boy in his rehab, who was a migrant worker in Johannesburg's sprawling construction business, murmured to him about a potential diamond mine near his village in the eastern part of Rhodesia (Zimbabwe). It was a small open-pit mine and known only to very few—just three families, which included his—who held it as a secret to avoid takeover by the government or by multinationals, as in Botswana, without any long-term benefits to the inhabitants of the area except exploited labour. He narrated that they had mined few stones which they had traded off secretly to mercenaries in neighbouring Mozambique, fearing suspicion and backlash from the government if they had become well off suddenly.

'We are ready to smuggle out the stones if our families are going to be rehabilitated in Europe or America with proper guarantee of regular jobs,' he confirmed, then added, 'I confided this only to you and no one else because I know you are trustworthy, and I'm very thankful for the way you look after our boys caringly, with you affording great personal sacrifice. Otherwise, they all would have ended up loitering the streets as looters and gangsters since we can't afford them proper upbringing and education. I'm thankful to you, truly.'

Johann van der Watt, a man admired for his tactical skill in the football field, was also a skilled technician in the physical execution of jobs. The way he acquired land in the suburb Melville and the subsequent launching of a highly regarded home for children of the poor without much hindrance of bureaucratic turpitude well known in the apartheid government proved his tactical skill beyond the football ground.

'We will work it out, and you all will be living a *king's* life soon,' Johann had said assuredly, patting the left shoulder of the man. No other assurances were needed. These few words conveyed the commitment—a commitment without a second thought—of the ever-reliable philanthropist.

The next following days were like days of tactical planning in a military war room of a country on the verge of going to war. Johann didn't have any military experience though. He hadn't even had the slightest thought about smuggling in his entire past life; football was his love and life until he moved down south to Joburg. Che's *Guerrilla Warfare*, which he had flipped through when he was in high school while preparing for a speech on leftist extremism in the school's annual symposium started to haunt him now. During those high school days, he had never thought that those unimaginable real-life situations described in the book would later on engulf him. He needed to get a hold of a copy so badly to explore the tactics anew—not for armed rebellion or surprise attack but for defensive activities against the attributes of military tactics in the book—and carry out smuggling activities unsuspected, undetected, and very clandestinely.

His bedroom walls, for the first time, was adorned with maps of (1) the African continent, (2) Rhodesia, (3) Mozambique, (4) South Africa, and (5) the largest and most prominent one, the map depicting the trio states of Rhodesia, Mozambique, and South Africa—a triangle drawn on it with a red marker pen, enveloping the shared border areas of the three states, which is similar to the Golden Triangle of Burma, Laos, and Thailand (the source of half the world's heroine drug) or the Bermuda Triangle (the most dreaded triangle for some supernatural reasons). The Triangle of Hope, he had named it—hope for the three families to embrace better lives in civilized society or for himself to reinvent his pro-poor ascetic life to a more enticingly pleasurable one. The triangle was the zone of operation for his smuggling activity that was supposedly military in nature.

The men of the three families were presently domiciled in Johannesburg, engaging in construction activities, as there was a drought-like situation back home. They had brought along some of their boys for helpers, but they had landed in Johann's home due to acute shortage of accommodation for boys and also due to the brutality of the atmosphere in the workers' colony, which was insidiously unfavourable for young boys to survive unscathed by drug abuse and other juvenile crimes.

Johann soon devised two angles of activity, or AoA in short, to smuggle out the stones to South Africa—the Mozambique angle and the direct-to-South-Africa angle.

The Mozambique angle would entail another beneficiary in the process, the Mozambican mercenaries, who would act as middlemen or simply as conduit in black-market parlance. This option had been partially tried and tested by Emmanuel and co. before and was successful. This had a higher chance of success, taking past precedence into consideration, but it meant a buy-back from the mercenaries for resale in Johannesburg or elsewhere, which would eventually erode a significant portion of the profits.

This meant selling the stones to the mercenaries first and asking them to sell back to them in South Africa or at another mutually agreed location. The greatest advantage was that there would be no loss even if the mercenaries were caught or intercepted by the police or border patrols since sales money would already be at hand, though comparatively smaller than the direct mines-to-market monopolistic sales money. If the mercenaries could safely trade with them in South Africa, it would be a double whammy—buying from them again, if they agreed, for further resale, escaping all the risks involved in transporting the goods to South Africa.

The direct-to-South-Africa angle was rife with high risks but blessed with wholesome profitability if successful. Here, the miners and the mercenaries were themselves. Everything from mining to transportation to sale depended entirely on them and, most of all, the security risk. The movement could be like (1) the strategic movement of arms, such as missiles and WMDs, by the federal army from one location to another, discreetly avoiding enemy and public attention, or (2) adoption of guerrilla warfare tactics in defensive mode to evade being waylaid by law enforcers from both countries. In spite of the heavy risks involved with the second AoA, the strategic-thinking mind of Johann still believed that the probable profitability outweighs the possible dangers.

After devising two strategic AoAs ready for adoption at any time, now he had to clear the groundwork to fulfil the precondition for cooperation laid out by Emmanuel—to rehabilitate the three families in Europe or America with the guarantee of proper livelihood. He chopped off America from the options right away without further consideration since he found it impossible or near to impossible for an ex-footballer from Europe to influence the administration there, where people were crazy about what he called *exotic* games—like basketball, baseball, and American football— but didn't have much regard for what they inappropriately called *soccer*. But when he thought about Europe, he felt he was spoilt by the variety of choices at hand—England, Denmark, France, and most of all, his own country, the Netherlands.

England was a good choice because his former manager at PSV, Sir Robert Hobson, was currently the manager of the legendary English club Arsenal. He felt he would be delighted to assist him if the families were branded as political victims with threats to their lives in the former British colony of Rhodesia. He also knew that the incumbent foreign secretary of UK was Sir Hobson's very close friend, whom he could influence easily or with some efforts. Another plus point was that Sir Hobson belonged to the constituency of the secretary of state for justice and lord chancellor, the Rt Hon. George Campbell.

Denmark was another huge prospect because of his mother's ancestry. She was a Danish of royal descent who was forced, together with her family, to seek refuge in Holland during the World War II because the downfall of Denmark to Nazi Germany would be disastrous, they presupposed, for the royal family and their immediate relatives due to the Schleswig plebiscites after World War I. He was confident that if his mother made a request—yes, on his behalf—to his cousins and nephews in the royal family of Denmark to talk to their government to consider the rehabilitation of just three distraught African families dislocated due to political reasons, it would be rather malicious on the part of the government not to accept such a meagre request from the royal family.

France was another potential destination because of the emerging political trend there with the resurgence of the Socialist Party, whose sympathizers vastly include the ex-servicemen and World War II veterans whom his father had fought along with as a soldier of the Allied Forces and still elaborately corresponded with. A request from his father to one of the veteran organizations there could catapult the message up to the political bosses in the Socialist Party, and the rehabilitation of just three political refugee families wouldn't be a daunting task, he presumed.

But the country holding the biggest potential success in his scheme of things was his very own country, the

Netherlands. His popularity there was enough to get him through the doors of the administration even without using any of his family's influence. He believed he could comfortably help sway the decision in his favour, being the recipient of—among the very few privileged sportspersons—the Order of the House of Orange, which was awarded by the country's monarch; the significance of his words would not simply dwindle down to oblivion in the corridors of the Ministry of the Interior and Kingdom Affairs, which had the upper hand among the ministries in granting asylum and political refuge.

After three days of weighing the pros and cons in each country, he finally chose the most desirable one, settling in favour of his own country, the Netherlands, among the various European countries he had weighed and measured. He immediately wrote a representation to the ambassador of the Netherlands in South Africa, at Pretoria, on the plight of the three families seeking refuge to the Netherlands due to political and ethnic reasons. He cited each and every detail of their future funding, which was meticulously prearranged, without the involvement of the state of the Netherlands under its social security scheme or policies on rehabilitation of refugees and asylum seekers. The financial burdens would partly be borne by the heads of the families, who would remain in Rhodesia, effectively in South Africa, and continue their struggle, with the support of some countries and organizations (including, least of all, Johann's rehab organization) sympathetic towards the sufferings of the ethnic minority groups.

The representation from a once well-loved Dutch footballer-turned-philanthropist now working for the underprivileged in South Africa was well received and endorsed by the ambassador.

'I was a huge fan of Feyenoord until recently when I shifted my loyalty to Ajax,' said the ambassador concordantly. 'I will forward the letter with my personal recommendation.'

The next thing that happened after the submission of the representation was the arrival of a correspondence from the junior minister in the Ministry of the Interior and Kingdom Affairs surprisingly allotting three grand family hostels near the port of Rotterdam, Johann's city of choice for the families, and requesting him to personally accompany them there and rehabilitate them initially with the state's help though Johann had cited in the representation that it was unequivocally not necessary. This happened just two weeks after Johann's representation. The approval was quick by any standard. Even the asylum request of a Libyan leader opposing the dictatorial rule of Muammar Gaddafi was not approved by the Dutch government this fast even though his life was in great danger and the situation called for great urgency.

The three families were moved down first to Johannesburg after carefully crafting their reason for leaving the village, so as not to leave behind any tinge of suspicion. The village headman was convinced that they were going to settle down in Joburg until the drought condition subsided at least minimally. However, the heads of the three families would often visit the village to stake their claim on their grazing and farming rights, which would otherwise be forfeited due to their long absence. This was another good reason to often move unsuspected into the village for the smuggling offensive purpose.

In Johannesburg, the families were accommodated at the rehab for the time being until they could be flown to the Netherlands. The paperwork and other issues involving immigration were abnormally smooth with the blessing and personal attention of the ambassador. Hardly after a week of their arrival in Johannesburg, they were flown to the Netherlands. The heads of the families accompanied their families but returned along with Johann to operationalize the plan for their future offensive.

Rotterdam City received them well, with the mayor personally dropping them off at their new accommodations. The children would attend a public school, and the ladies would be provided unskilled jobs in the nearby port after their completion of basic training mainly for safety and protocol purposes. Johann's father would take personal responsibility for their well-being as their local guardian. After successfully rehabilitating the families in Rotterdam, the precondition for implementation of the strategies was accomplished, earning Johann the 'right to trade' with the three Rhodesian villagers as per their precondition, and their confidence as well. So far so good.

Now the offensive part should begin. The most daunting part was training the three men, and himself in handling firearms—not that they were going to fight a guerrilla warfare, but they needed to arm themselves for self-defence purposes. Johann purchased four *Chinese-made* Glock pistols from a seasoned Chinese overseas merchant who was rumoured to be the man who had armed the anti-apartheid revolutionaries in South Africa.

The training looked daunting and impractical because any echo of pistol shooting in the city limits would be too risky an affair, looking at the prevailing volatile political situation, and moreover, attracting the attention of the authorities at this time could vouch failure in the operational strategy later on. The most viable place for training was the vicinity of Witwatersrand with its sporadic gold-mining activities and seclusion from dense human habitation. Even here, choosing the farm in the surroundings for the training activity had to be done while keeping ethnicity in mind. Training with three black men in firearms in a white man's farm could unnecessarily provoke the suspicion of the farm owner that he was training to arm black people for anti-apartheid revolution. It should be on a black man's farm.

This made him choose the farm of Raymond Zulu, who was once a political prisoner for going against the white supremacist regime. He had inherited a vast tract of family land near Witwatersrand. Johann had known Raymond when he made a surprise visit to his rehab to appreciate his work for the children of poor black labourers. After the visit, they had bonded well as good friends, and Johann van der Watt paid intermittent visits to Raymond's farm mostly on public holidays and weekends.

Raymond Zulu as an anti-apartheid revolutionary was no stranger to the use of firearms, which proved thickly providential to Johann van der Watt, making his job of hunting a trainer in using firearms less intricate. The search for a firearm coach stopped in the farm itself, which made the choice of the farm more obvious, and lucrative. The training session was improvised in such a way that even Raymond Zulu was not apprehensive of the actual purpose. There was no requirement of tactical training in the farm; it was for firearm usage. The tactical part was taken care of in the rooms of Johann's rehab in a type of classroom teaching typical to a military theoretical session. The tactical part perhaps included the secretive commando-type entry and movement in a foreign land, the intermingling with the village people (though minimally), the secluded mining activity, and the smuggling out of the stones from Rhodesia to the point of sales in Johannesburg.

The gunfire training sessions at Raymond Zulu's farm went off smoothly after two week-long sessions with no untoward alarm being set off since, as stated, the area was concomitant with reverberant sounds of mining activities.

Well set, they set off for an expedition but with no intention of smuggling; they wanted to survey the topography of the route they so proposed to tread, to anticipate potential dangers, and to identify probable escape routes in times of threats. Emmanuel and friends had been using this route to move up and down Johannesburg from their village and were quite well-versed about it, no doubt. But for a mission so fragile and tensive, just possessing knowledge about the route up and down was not enough; each and every strategic point had to be identified and studied carefully.

The expedition was led by Johann van der Watt. The team comprised of three other men: Emmanuel and his friends Mufumu and Farai. They crossed the South Africa–Rhodesia border from the irregular frontiers not manned by border guards on both sides along the Limpopo River close to the Botswana border. They entered Tuli, then Fort Victoria (Masvingo), then Chipinga, the nearest town on the periphery of Emmanuel's village of Gumira, where diamonds were supposedly to be mined and smuggled out.

There were few military checkpoints en route but causing no hindrance to movements of vehicles. This was one point to be observed again on their return to ascertain whether it was just for the time being that they were casual in their functioning and approach. From Chipinga, they were real foot soldiers scaling the hill slopes on the unfamiliar jungle roads on the way to the secret mining area not so far away from Gumira.

The location of the mine, a hinterland near the low-lying hills not so far away from Gumira village on the eastern side towards Mozambique, was a secluded place because of its harsh features suitable only for reptiles to survive. The grasses here were scattered and looked freckled like the shrubs in sub-Saharan vegetation. It was not endowed with streams or lakes or any other water bodies to support vegetation growth or large-scale farming or grasslands for cattle's feed. The expanse looked like a landform of great archaeological fascination that could mine cauldrons of bones from mammals and reptiles of the Jurassic period. That look indeed was the evidence of the likely presence of diamonds, as time-tested wisdom of diamond mining would tell. The thin crust of soil was the cover of the igneous rocks beneath, known by early South African miners as kimberlites, whose potential content of ores (aka diamond) was hauntingly significant.

They were satisfied with the onward journey. They had explored the environment of the mine and did a trial digging to test the viability of the mine, discovering a sparkling ore within a few hours of digging. They then carefully buried the ore in the mine again and hid the whole mine, allowing it to blend in with its surroundings. Johann van der Watt formally commissioned the launch of the mission with a salute to the fading sun and loud applause from his friends, and then he ordered a retreat for their return journey, like a military retreat after a successful exercise, a real onslaught awaiting to prune the area of its rich resources.

The return journey also went off smoothly without stumbling on any physical hindrance; they followed the same line as the onward journey, studying intently the pattern of people's movements and the functioning of the military checkpoints. The checkpoints were fortunately minimal in activities, just a symbolic presence regulating and identifying vehicles plying on the state highways. There were no stopping of vehicles and frisking of passengers.

However, the biggest doubt in Johann's mind was not about physical hindrances but mental ones that could pose a threat to the mission. He was doubtful if they all could display the same cool attitude and be sagacious enough to avoid confrontation if they were strapped with diamonds on their bodies, which could cause jittery and mental stress easily; a slightest display of awkwardness could lead to suspicion and, worse, apprehension.

Now their journey was like a joyride; everyone knew awfully well that there was nothing illegal attached to them and their body was clean, so they were mentally calm to freely interact with other people. Pistols were hidden in their inners; however, they were not a cause for worry but rather a norm in a land infested with RENAMO militants from neighbour Mozambique supported by the Rhodesian government. Johann understood that the mental hindrance would pose a greater threat than physical hindrance. He had had reasonable experience about mental stress as a professional football player knowing quite well the skills displayed in the practice field were not always adaptable in the jam-packed stadium.

The expedition was successful with no intrusive obstacles on the way. The route was clear and verified, and the veracity of the mine had also been tested and established right. The way ahead was just mining and safe transportation, followed by a meticulous trade-off with equitable profit sharing.

Having jiggled through the preliminary exercise unhindered, the first expedition for exploration was undertaken soon with Johann van der Watt at the lead again. This time, even following the same route as the trial expedition did bring a feverish atmosphere to each team member, and they unknowingly displayed nervousness in their expressions, facial and physical, unlike the jovial expressions with the joyride expedition. This was only the onward journey, with no diamonds strapped yet on their bodies, but the aura of nervousness, blended with a slight feeling of excitement, was already looming large.

They arrived at the mining area by sunset and set up tents, hiding them as much as possible near the open-pit mine which Emmanuel and friends had dug up earlier and which was dug up again for the experimental mining during the trial expedition. According to schedule, mining was to be done only at dawn till sunrise, followed by a siesta to bypass the infernal noontime temperature. They would survey the landscape in the afternoon with the dual intention of examining the minability of the surroundings and to delude any passersby (though their appearance was unlikely, but the chances of this happening were unpredictable) of their real intention by briefing them of a survey for water tables in the area for possible drilling to quench the hinterland and turn it into an arable one.

The digging and panning for the sparkle was judiciously proceeded, confining it in as small an area as possible and not spreading it wide across the field to avoid detection of the mining activities by the villagers. After five days of digging and panning within a few square meters, a few diamond ores were mined. Though large enough in quantity to make favourable returns, they were suitably small in number and size to be strapped to human bodies to avoid detection by simple observation or glancing. The process of the mining was carried out in such a way that the excavation was always followed by the filling up of the pit after reaching five to seven metres deep whether an ore was found or not after panning and careful segregation.

It was meticulously planned so that those proven mines could be dug up again in future expeditions going beyond five to seven metres deep with improved implements and processes. No open mine was left in the end to unnecessarily provoke suspicion by any human being who could pass by the area. Another advantage was that this area had not been known for mining activity of any kind, nor was it classified as a potential area for mining, just a hinterland unattractive for any human activity of economic scale, agrarian or industrial, and most unsuitable for human habitation.

CHAPTER 11

After almost two years of successful exploitation of the area and after gaining rich dividends that would entitle him to lead an ostentatiously enviable lifestyle for the rest of his life, Johann van der Watt understood that their dacoit-like activity of clandestine mining could not continue undetected. The danger loomed larger since the area bordering Mozambique had now largely been controlled by rebels fighting against the white people–led government covering most of today's Manicaland. They had sighted many a times, at a distance though, the patrols of irregular soldiers of the rebels belonging to the recently regrouped ZANU, who based their struggle in camps inside Mozambique. They would be more unforgiving than the regular armies of the government, charging them with stealing the valuable resources of their land which they too were yet to discover. Recent incidents revealed how rudely they had behaved to detractors and captured government soldiers, torturing them in the most inhumane of manners. It was a real threat necessitating abortion of the illegal mining activity in toto.

Johann van der Watt herded together his lieutenants, Emmanuel and co., at his office chamber for a serious discussion one Sunday afternoon. That was already two months after their last expedition, which was the most successful one; a celebration of their last haul still lingered in their minds. Emmanuel and friends were also already apprehensive about the successful continuation of the smuggling activity. They were satisfied with what they had gained and preferred to cease the activity to lead normal lives with their families. With all their earnings during the two adventurous years, they would have enough resources to enjoy a privileged lifestyle and support themselves in times of trouble when they joined their families in the Netherlands, or otherwise, they could lead a normal middle-class life supported by another regular income in working as unskilled labour much in demand in the port of Rotterdam even if the larger share of their bounties could not be retrieved there at once. More than bringing back their families to Africa (South Africa or Rhodesia), they preferred to settle down in the developed and peaceful environment of the West. So even if they were unable to retrieve their huge earnings in bulk due to potential interception by authorities in the Netherlands, they preferred to carry it in trickles, keeping in the custody of Johann their earnings from the diamond mercenary. They all unanimously decided to call it quits.

However, the farewell to his faithful soldiers seemed to be just the beginning of a new chapter in Johann's smuggling activity. He had never imagined that his knowledge of the diamond mines in Rhodesia would eventually benefit much of the marginalized black majority of Rhodesia in their military struggle against the rule of the white minority. This was the time when Robert Mugabe had taken the lead role in the fight against the rule of the white minority under the flagship organization Zimbabwe African National Union (ZANU). Robert Mugabe had been camping in bases in Mozambique, regrouping the splintered militants and mobilizing resources. Mobilizing financial resources for procurement of arms and ammunitions and rations for the revolutionary soldiers was the most critical agenda of the resurrected union and most crucial to the success of their prolonged struggle.

It was at this critical juncture that Johann van der Watt chanced upon a meeting with the main fundraiser for Mugabe one weekend in one of his usual visits to his long-time friend Raymond Zulu at his farm near Witwatersrand. Raymond Zulu had always been sympathetic towards the plight of the Rhodesian black majority. He was also a crusader in South Africa for the greater role of the black majority in politics and administration. Johann realized no amount of his contributable fund would benefit the ZANU in their long-drawn-out war. So he wanted to help them source regular funds to continue their struggle unhindered and tidily satisfy behind the scene his thirst for continuing the diamond trade.

The fundraiser was David Midzi, a former investment banker from New York. He was the second son of a hugely popular Rhodesian freedom fighter and writer. After acquiring a law degree from the University of Chicago, he joined Columbia Business School for an MBA course. An MBA degree from the elite school instantly landed him in a high-profile job at Merrill Lynch & Co., and he had a successful stint there for about five years before he quit the job to become a militant and a patriot for the emancipation of the black majority in Rhodesia.

While working for Merrill Lynch, David Midzi had met Robert Mugabe, who came to New York to deliver a speech at a UN convention. Robert Mugabe had pleaded with him to join him in the struggle in the land of their forefathers to deliver their people from the clutches of the ruthless rule of the white minority. Initially, David was reluctant to join the struggle and surrender his comfortable lifestyle in New York, where he earned handsomely enough to enjoy two overseas holidays a year. He would have to settle and unconvincingly be satisfied with just two meals a day in the militants' camps, and that too was extraordinarily a luxury, with the prevailing tight supply situation and financial position. The patriotism in his blood won him over at the end, and he went revolutionary, leaving behind the high-paying job and the luxury of being a part of the high-class New York society.

Johann confronted David Midzi if his organization wanted him to donate a meagre one-time contribution of a few thousand dollars or to lead them to an eternal source of funds to continue their fight against the minority regime until victory was at hand. The latter choice was obvious, believed David Midzi, if it was out of the rightful mind of a true sympathizer. He was not expecting to see the corporeal manifestation of Aries, the god of war, in the form of an ex-footballer-turned-philanthropist. It was hard to believe, yes. Or else, his reservation went, was it a clever trick to lead them blindfolded on the path to surrender via the corridor of greed, knowing their greatest weakness lay in the financial front? Could there be anything like an unhindered flow of funds from any source for the black people fighting against a white regime when garnering support from the international community was never easy even without asking for financial support? David was ambivalent about the offer.

David Midzi reacted thoughtfully, 'As a former investment banker, I know that the greatest goods come from the challenges with the greatest risks. No reward is more enticing than the ones that come out of the bruises of life-threatening risks. I do not know who you are to trust you wholeheartedly and stuff my full basket of faith into. But today, out of hope for brighter days for my people tomorrow, I repose my faith in you unconditionally that you will lead us to the source of money to liberate the black people of Rhodesia. I wish this unconditional trust won't fail me and the people of Rhodesia.'

The declaration proclaimed the beginning of the greatest excavation of the soils of Rhodesia in history. The purpose—the rejuvenation of the much-disrupted mass struggle against minority misrule.

With the support of the incumbent government in Mozambique, the diamonds of Rhodesia were freely exported from the port of Beira under the extraordinary supervision of Johann van der Watt, who had established healthy contacts in Asia, mostly in India, and would not relent easily to diktats from foreign agencies (read the West).

The trade was carried out with or without Johann at Beira. He sometimes remotely dictated the trading patterns from Johannesburg, with his emphasis on the orphanage he had founded for the black vagabonds. With the liberating forces gaining ground in Rhodesia, Johann gradually directed his heart more on the children in his orphanage home. That was when Jonathan Tobi arrived at Johannesburg upon Johann's invitation. And that sowed the beginning of the chapter when the diamond trade of the Rhodesian mercenaries was going to be diverged by an unexpected turn, bending the trade more to the benefit of the few warlords.

CHAPTER 12

After a brief stint at Witwatersrand Backpacker Lodge at Hillbrow, Jonathan Tobi moved to the hostel of Johann van der Watt to start his internship in the great art of trading diamonds in the black market. Johann had started re-establishing himself as a selfless volunteer for taking care of the children of black migrants, who were mostly in the shanty towns of Johannesburg. Meanwhile, he had the privilege of running a widely successful fundraising campaign for the struggle in Rhodesia in the form of diamond trade with the black Rhodesian militants.

This latter activity was where he wanted to shed his fat on though; the proliferating dividends were seductive, with not much risk involved. Unlike the days with Emmanuel and co., it was now being supported by a strong militant organization in need of a regular flow of funds and the federal government in Mozambique contented with the transit royalty. Now he wanted to play a mentor role instead, a role less obligating but not less sublime, and delegate the functional role to a man capable enough to be the liaison between the source functionaries and the market.

Jonathan Tobi was courteously happy to be the right hand of the untamed diamond baron, the role he had longed for and had been fantasizing about for years. His great attention to details and his interpersonal skills soon earned the confidence of the baron, who needed a reliable man to succeed him to continue the fundraising activity of the union waging a prolonged war with the minority white rulers in Rhodesia. His brisk and robust build and his lineage, that of a Jewish trading family seasoned by Indian culture, aptly made Jonathan Tobi more suitable for the challenging job. The deterioration of his health condition and mobility due to the unexpected onset of Huntington's disease did not permit Johann to cling on to the role with the risk of being apprehended by the South African authorities—but only due to his declining capability and nothing else—which would be an extreme embarrassing situation.

Then at Beira, being along with Johann van der Watt, Jonathan had first-hand experiences on the logistical processes and, most importantly, the privilege of being acknowledged as the heir apparent to the baron, who would retire shortly to be with his children in the rehab full-time.

In a few months, Jonathan Tobi became the man who took the most critical of decisions in Beira, which had been assertively the prerogative of Johann van der Watt before. His ascension to the role was not catapulted by Johann; he himself had earned it. This was when the support of the government of Mozambique was eroding fast and the source of the most crucial fund for the union fighters was at stake.

The government of Mozambique, under constant pressure from friends of the white people–led government of Rhodesia, unexpectedly released an official order to the militias operating within its soil to not indulge in subversive activities and illegal transportation of natural resources. The order was not in so harsh a tone but was detrimental enough to the Rhodesian rebels, causing concern among the leaders on whether continuing the illegal diamond trade would further hamper their relationship with the Mozambican government.

At this point in time, a good or even partly cordial relationship with the Mozambican government was the only plausible lifeline of the union fighting against the minority regime in Rhodesia, and the diamond trade was the only regular source of funding war expenses. The debates among leaders on whether to stop the trade and go begging to some foreign countries again or to carry on and invoke the ire of the Mozambican government caused them to totally quit the activity and also vacate camps inside the country; this situation occurred shortly after Jonathan Tobi took charge of the trade in Beira.

He knew that only greater sacrifices could earn back the confidence and favour of the Mozambican government. The Mozambican government should not only earn transit royalties from the diamond trade. They should play a greater role by directly or indirectly participating in the trade and earning a bigger income from it. Meanwhile, the Mozambican government was also struggling for want of funds. This would mean greater sacrifices from the union militants for now, but the trade would grow manifold after some time if and only if the Mozambican government agreed to join hands for partnership. Jonathan Tobi believed that more compromises now would come with better patronage in the process and more income in the long run.

His target right away was the defence minister of Mozambique, who too was a warlord once and was now the number two in the regime. His advocacy for greater funding to the military for greater stability in the country and the region as a whole had earned him the confidence of his generals and the admiration of the people. He was an avid shopper for military hardware abroad, with regular kickbacks trickling into his Swiss bank accounts concurrently. If he would like to participate in the trade, with one of his trusted generals deputed as his pointsman, the army would have another regular source of income, which would also augur well for its modernization plan without a deep-rooted dependence on the sovereign budget and would also compensate the habitual shopping expenses of its defence minister for weapons abroad.

Jonathan Tobi assumed that this ambitious mindset of the defence minister would make him more vulnerable to be won over before anyone could think a way out. With his assessment of the present government in Mozambique and his analysis of each minister, he independently came to the conclusion that the defence minister was not peculiarly corruption personified, but his ambitions for the modernization of the military and a greater role for the Mozambican government in the region made him susceptible to outsiders' influence. His receiving of kickbacks in arms purchases were not of his asking but was a tradition in the military hardware bazaar as a show of gratitude to valued clients, primarily for retention purpose. This practice had enslaved him gradually and made him exponentially gullible to Western arms manufacturers, who later on unflinchingly induced him with gifts to sweeten deals or to secure military contracts.

When Jonathan Tobi met the minister, he did outline the benefits the Mozambican government—or precisely, the military—would receive by being a partner in the trade by way of granting free movement and the usage of Beira port unconditionally and sending a representative to oversee the trade. He also mentioned very prominently the benefits the defence minister would personally reap—not immediately, but in the long run—most probably when the war in Rhodesia was won by the union. Jonathan Tobi promised to be his long-term business partner even without the participation of Rhodesian militants and the Mozambican government.

'Most of all, it's a personal deal between you and me for our future partnership. The time will come soon when you and I together will control a vast chunk of the diamond trade in Africa. We are entitled to receive this grandeur for our selfless service,' said Jonathan Tobi enthusiastically to give personal assurance to the minister.

The Mozambican government participated as a partner, as advised by its defence minister, having as his proxy one major general posted as representative officer in the trade office of the Rhodesian militants in Beira. The trade swung back to the usual business but was more secure and stronger in intensity than before with the indirect participation of the government of the host country. Diamond mines near the Gumira area were to be the precursors to the discovery of one of present day's largest diamond mines—the Marange mines.

At this time, Jonathan had started scouting for a location to control and redirect the Southern African diamond trade from Eastern Africa. This would give him strategic advantage when the hordes of union militants headed back to Rhodesia, abandoning the diamond trade and leaving it to the mercy of the few dissolute warlords to clandestinely carry on with help from men loyal to the defence minister of Mozambique. He wanted a place presenting the most unsuspicious of environments for illegal diamond trade but having a stable government viable to carry out a profitable local business in pretext to deter suspicion for his real business concern. After his hunt for the ideal location, he settled on Nairobi, the capital of Kenya, which had good access to the port of Mombasa.

Kenya by that time had become the cradle of modern civilization in Eastern Africa, with a stable democratic government under President Daniel arap Moi, who succeeded to the presidency after the death of Jomo Kenyatta, the first president under the new republic declared in 1964.

Jonathan had another undeniable reason for choosing Nairobi—the presence of large swathes of Gujarati migrants whom Jonathan could claim as his acquaintances very comfortably. After all, his first language being Gujarati, he was a Jew only by descent. Moreover, his business partners in Bombay—his buyers, in fact—were mostly Gujaratis. They were the ones who absorbed the bulk of his business—the militants' business, to be precise. He couldn't value his Indian market more than anything else.

CHAPTER 13

Jonathan Tobi was right in scouting for a safer location from where to control the diamond trade away from Mozambique a few months after he took over the mantle from Johann van der Watt. He believed that after the union militants made deeper inroads into Rhodesia and if a ceasefire was finally agreed upon, the diamond trade would be lulled to an almost non-existence for a time. That would bring forth the birth of splinter organizations dissatisfied by the development; history would repeat itself. He needed to tap this opportunity but not, under any circumstances, from within their jurisdiction, so he would be able to control the trade independently and not let himself come under their control.

Under his pressure and the alibi that there was a need for major funding of the war when it was at its peak and victory was at sight, the last two months before the ceasefire saw the greatest hours of excavations and the largest shipment of rough diamonds, and his share of fortune upped unprecedentedly, which he cleverly parked far away in Kenya and India. However, he was yet undecided in leaving Beira.

The ceasefire happened soon, as Jonathan had expected, and was subsequently followed by the establishment of a biracial democracy in Rhodesia, which heralded greater participation of the black majority in governance and many of the political leaders of the black rebels taking up important assignments in government and public offices. However, the continuation of sanctions on trade robbed the government of the capacity to absorb or pacify and rehabilitate handsomely the pro-black fighters variously commanded by warlords of different regions. The situation was worsened by the participation of the union leaders in the subsequent election of 1980 without taking their commanders, the mainstay of the revolution, into confidence. This was the last warning for Jonathan to leave southern Africa and take shelter in his newfound abode, Nairobi. After the election of 1980, the trade came to a standstill.

The warlord controlling the land bordering Mozambique in the south-east was among the disgruntled lot and the strongest of union's commanders. His name was Peter Kabweza, a revolutionary with Che Guevara's trait, highly motivated for the cause of establishing power for the black majority and usurping the white minority's regime. His main discontent was not about the insufficient monetary compensation or dispensation but on the establishment of a biracial democracy in Rhodesia, his beloved country. He had hoped for a black-majority rule in Rhodesia without the participation of the white minority, who had had misruled his country for years. Even if allowed, they should be exclusively elected on universal franchise and without special reservation for them, which meant only a trickle would represent them without much say in the legislature. His dream was summarily shattered by the defiance of the leaders who accepted the biracial democracy and the union's participation in the election of 1980 without consensus.

In the meantime, the Rhodesian election and the consequential positive developments in Rhodesia created an unprecedented vacuum in the financing of the military in Mozambique, whose budgetary dependence had momentarily been subsided with their proxy participation in the diamond trade. This situation could backfire into popular discontent among the generals and even the foot soldiers, which would necessitate cutting their privileges from housing to housekeeping. This would invariably erode the popularity of the defence minister, causing him to lose his strong grip on the commanding generals, whom he had charmed with good livelihood and lifestyle, which had been partly inexistent in the military history of Mozambique before.

This *stagflation*-like condition was the crisis Jonathan Tobi had foreseen, and he had mounted a meticulous plan to take advantage of it by shifting his base from Beira to Nairobi soon after the election of 1980. He had scouted for a safe haven when he sensed that development in Rhodesia was moving towards settlement and that it was no longer in his best interest to hole up in Beira. By the time the stagflation-like situation appeared, covering the discontented Rhodesian warlords and Mozambique's military, he was already luxuriously running a parallel business in Kenya. If he had still been holing up in Beira, he would have been under Mozambique's military control and probably subjugation and possible utilization as a second-hand partner by the disenchanted warlords, who would want to smuggle out diamonds from Rhodesia to reengage with the struggle.

Now in Nairobi, he was the messiah for the two groups, who would seek his divine intervention for charting regular inflow of funds for (1) re-enacting the rebellious freedom struggle for the Rhodesians and (2) supplementing the budgetary support for Mozambique's military spending to generally maintain the status quo lifestyle of the generals.

Hence, the trade from Beira had another intersection now—Kenya. Every piece of ore shipped out from Beira was directed first to Mombasa port to the care of Jonathan Tobi's men. The mining and transportation of the ores from Rhodesia to Beira were at the hands of the Rhodesian warlords led by Peter Kabweza. From Beira, they would be under the military facilities and undertakings.

Nairobi, the capital, served as the business hub, with the vast presence of Gujarati migrants providing good ready-to-use emissaries for traders in Bombay and Surat. Jonathan Tobi seldom sent the goods directly to India. Nairobi was his point of sales (or simply POS) at large. This was before his emotional engagement with *liaison*, which would necessitate him to personally get involved in supplying roughs to his Indian partners.

Both the Rhodesian and the Mozambican groups received the trade proceeds directly from Jonathan Tobi. It didn't matter how he redirected or utilized the diamonds or how he bargained for the price in the market; he immediately arranged for payments according to the predetermined price, dividing the shares of the two groups when the goods reached his safe haven. This speedy settlement created a high level of confidence in JT among the different players, Peter Kabweza, and the military authorities in Mozambique. In fact, he was now transformed into a buyer for them from being the seller of their goods in the international diamond bazaar. The trade sailed smoothly.

There was no untoward incident encountered in the trade cycle even after three long years of their association until an incident of piracy knocked them down almost to eternal enmity. It was when a shipment of ores from Beira encountered a very daunting and unexpected challenge; a huge consignment, along with the ship, vanished in the sea unexpectedly and simply became untraceable. This led to the realization and discovery of the resurrection of the dreaded Somalian pirates in the seas adjoining the Horn of Africa to the south till Tanzania. The repercussion of this heavy loss was so enormous it almost entirely disbanded their association in the fight for legitimacy of claims and counterclaims.

The contention of Peter Kabweza was that the goods had been delivered to the safe hands of the Mozambican military, and so he had to be compensated for the loss. His or his party's role was the safe delivery of the goods to the facilities of the Mozambican military. The Mozambican military also constructed their counterclaim, stating that loading the goods in their commonly accepted shipping company's ship, which bore a Panamanian flag but was administered from Beira, and flagging it off to the sea was their sole responsibility.

The shipping company was actually the surrogate concern of Mozambique's army for its unholy arms acquisition from middlemen acting on behalf of Eastern European governments and their accredited weapon manufacturers. The Panamanian registration meant that the ships are devoid of the company of guards from the Mozambican military, but on the other hand, it hid the dirty activities undertaken under its guise. A military insider had once termed the company as the torchbearer of African revolution, under whose flag Mozambique had discreetly supported tremendous rebellious movements in the continent with a supply of arms and ammunitions.

These arguments for claims and counterclaims were raised and fought over even before Jonathan Tobi made his position known on the vexing issue. They were pre-emptive in nature and speculative in appearance and short-sighted in purpose. If Jonathan Tobi were to decline paying any consignments until the goods were delivered to his safe custody, this entailed that they were sure losers in the tragedy—the greatest being the Rhodesian revolutionaries under Peter Kabweza and, to a lesser extent but psychologically greater still, the military of Mozambican government, whose credibility and capability to ship the ores were eroded since the people running the company were its men.

The resurrection of the Somalian pirates created an unbridled security situation in large parts of the Arabian Sea, which adjoined countries from Somalia till Tanzania; it was volatile enough that floating armouries of private security agencies were engaged by companies trading and voyaging significantly in the eastern shore of Africa, especially since the incident of the Mozambican shipping company's loss came to light. The darkest part was that the pirates didn't make any attempt to contact the shipping company or the government of Mozambique for ransom or negotiation for monetary or political support, showing total disregard for human lives if enough loot had been garnered. The loss of the ship was acknowledged after frantic calls to the ship went unanswered a day after it was due to arrive at Mombasa. The loot, it was assumed, was large enough to satisfy the pirates to remain gleefully silent and not undertake further demands.

The ship was lost, and so were her crew and the twelve small parcels of highly priced diamond ores she carried along other visibly bulky trading items just for sake of hiding the real valuable consignments. As much as its concern for the ship, the Mozambican government could not initiate comprehensive search-and-rescue operations, if it had been viable at the time, because of the registration tag of the ship. The crew was Mozambican in identity, but the ship was Panamanian in recognition. The defence circle of Mozambique suspected that the lack of contact from the pirates for ransom or political demands was due to the diamond parcels in the ship. After finding the precious ores, the pirates must have been highly elated to sail back directly to their sanctuary after sinking the ship and the men, leaving no trail or chance of being surrounded and captured by navy ships patrolling the area if the detaining was prolonged. The most striking area of security concern was how the ship was captured without any chance for the crew to raise an alarm or an SOS in any form, visual or electronic. It was a total blanket capturing.

Peter Kabweza adamantly demanded that if his loss was not compensated, he wouldn't deal with the Mozambican military any more. He would circumvent them and would send the ores directly to Jonathan Tobi or somewhere else in Asia. He threatened the Mozambican military to compensate him handsomely, or otherwise, he would sever all forms of ties, political and business. The Mozambican government was in no mood to compensate a loss, which too had a great bearing on them, jolting their credibility as a seafaring nation and as a safe custodian between the source and the market of the diamond trade among the three parties. The loss of the consignment was immense in monetary terms but greater still in terms of business reliability, rocking the very ethos of their long association and leading to a new, unwelcomed chapter—trust deficit. The term set by the Mozambican military in retaliation was 'Get lost and leave our land forever.' That meant Peter Kabweza's short-sightedness would not only let him lose the payment in totality but also his much-coveted support system and refuge.

The recriminations were bitterly mutual. The situation was encumbering.

The long-stalled peace process, the redundant international interventions in Somalia, the outbreak of civil war and more local revolts and instability, and Somalians resorting to local forms of conflict resolution due to the absence of a central government had instigated an atmosphere conducive to the emergence of seafaring robbers. The country had the longest coastline in Africa.

Until the ship *Estrela*, which bore the Panamanian flag, of the company controlled by the Mozambican military vanished in the seas bordering Tanzania while carrying parcels of rough diamonds among others, there were no notable incidents of piracy in the seas south of Kenya. Till then, the activities of the Somalian pirates were concentrated in the Gulf of Aden and, to some extent, southernmost to the northern Kenyan waters.

Estrela, meaning 'star' in Portuguese, was the pride of the company and a star performer in deep-sea trade, complementing the military's policy. It had sojourned to different hemispheres in the continent with its political agendum, supporting many revolutionary armies with a supply of arms purchased by the Mozambican military from middlemen of Eastern European origins. It was the largest and fastest of the five ships owned by the company and, since its inception, had been commanded by a voluntarily retired colonel of the Mozambican army. It was a Flower-class corvette purchased second-hand from the Royal Canadian Navy, refitted, and modified for commercial usage.

The *Estrela* episode could have snowballed into an irreconcilable breakdown of the relationship between Peter Kabweza and the Mozambican military, heralding the unnatural death of the struggle for black supremacy in Rhodesia, the struggle humbly but almost single-handedly still carried on by Peter Kabweza, with funds that trickle down from just one source—the diamond trade. The military ambition of Mozambique in the region would be severely impaired and dented as well, and the ambitions of the defence minister would be summarily subdued; and also, in the process, there was a certain likelihood that Jonathan Tobi's business empire would be severely impacted had his intervention at that ripe moment not been recognizably sacrificial. The action was interestingly epic.

Jonathan Tobi, who grew up with an art he had so notoriously employed in seducing beautiful girls from his neighbourhood, had long understood that man's willingness to take extreme steps was not due to frustration or cowardice, as most people assumed it to be. Nor was it lack of confidence to deal with the situation that had always necessitated taking steps that were extreme in nature. It was mostly foresight blurred with self-pity and injustice that hurled men to actions myopically extreme without caring for the outcome.

So instilling self-confidence with genuine concern and wiping out the sense of loss even with monetary compensation, if necessary, could be of great help in mitigating the disaster. This was true even in the case of love. Jonathan Tobi had employed this knowledge in luring girls of his choice during the era of his youthful debaucheries in the Katargam locality of Surat. He had said imbibing a sense of importance in the minds of the girls in very high degrees but tacitly with a tender approach most favourably resulted in longings and cravings for more concern. And that was how that thing called love would blossom among the young bloods.

He knew the revolutionaries, with years of underground stints, did yearn for tender care too, like young girls entering adolescence and attaining the permissible age to desire and experience tenderly care—it was truly a habit of human beings—of the opposite sex. Indeed, they would have seen this dramatically displayed in the public domain, from older friends, and in films and novels. Likewise, the revolutionaries longed for genuine care and concern in the form of recognition and acceptance at large given their insecurity and secluded lifestyle.

Jonathan Tobi had theoretically summed up this tendency of young girls and the revolutionaries together: 'Give them bread, and they will give you breath.'

He devised a plan to control the misunderstanding arising out of the loss of *Estrela* not from out of nowhere but from the spring of his learned knowledge from his youthful (mis)adventures. 'Give them bread, and they will give you breath.'

His plan's details were as follows: Peter Kabweza would be compensated for the exact amount of his loss, provided he would not make any ulterior demands in the future if any recurrence of loss occurred in the high seas. He would contribute 15 per cent of his total receipts to the company to help them procure a new vessel. This will last till the eighth shipment in the future. The Mozambican military wouldn't be compensated directly, but Jonathan Tobi would broker a deal for the company to purchase a second-hand vessel at a throwaway price, likely from the Kenyan Navy. The Kenyan government had retired a few patrol crafts of the erstwhile Royal East African Navy after the formation of the Kenyan Navy due to rising maintenance costs and old age. The vessel would then be registered in Mozambique and would bear a Mozambican flag so that the encumbrances of the *Estrela* episode would not recur. The Mozambican military would provide authentic escorts to the ship if the need arose, even posting armed navy personnel aboard.

All in all, Jonathan Tobi would bear all the loss and the trouble of shopping for a new vessel. The plan was mutually accepted. Bad blood was reverted after the brief fiasco.

CHAPTER 14

Jonathan's reappearance in the long-stalled diamond trade ushered in a new impetus, a kind of spiritual renaissance, to the Indian diamond market. It sparked an inertia of optimism for monumental growth once again being provided with another regular flow of ores from the *shadowy* African mines, which had already been forgotten after its long dormancy after a few years of ceasefire between the union and the government of Rhodesia. It had once been instrumental in controlling the unmitigated price hike by the South African exporters as they hoarded up ores to drive a hard bargain and maximize their gains. The Indian purchasers could now build up their stock of ores again, courtesy of Mr JT, to thwart any provocative actions from the South African miners and hence establish price stability. This resurrection of the almost-extinct trading pattern accorded Jonathan Tobi an indelible mark of respect among the Indian diamond traders, bestowing on him a strong clout of influence in the market that was unparalleled and unprecedented.

So was the case in Africa. His importance had risen phenomenally with the complete dependence of the Rhodesian rebels and the Mozambican military on him for sales of rough diamonds, especially after his successful intervention—with dignity, not rancour—in the Somalian piracy fiasco. The Mozambican military couldn't directly sell the illegal ores sourced from Rhodesia to anywhere else except to Jonathan Tobi since it would undermine its sovereign status and international commitments. It would be hazardous for a sovereign state to openly sell blood diamonds in the international market. The rebels under Peter Kabweza would not be able to continue their struggle either without the continued patronization of the Mozambican army and, most importantly, the indirect participation of Jonathan Tobi in facilitating the illicit diamond trade.

The diamond trade from Nairobi was the confluence of two contrasting elements that manifested in unison: beneficiary-cum-benefactor. Apart from the defence minister of Mozambique and Peter Kabweza, there was another outstanding but intangible beneficiary-cum-benefactor—the politics of Kenya. The smooth sailing of the illegal trade was possible due to Jonathan's generosity in funding political events behind the scene, mostly of the ruling party and several of the fractured opposition. However, this funding was secretly conducted, acknowledged only by the few powerful bosses who were at the helm of political affairs of the country and under massive public exposure and scrutiny. They were in a position most inappropriate to extract public money but were in great need of resources to fund their political ambitions. In return, this bartered mileage of favours to Jonathan Tobi from the two poles of Kenyan politics. Even then, he had never attempted to interfere in the affairs and governance of the ruling and the opposition parties. This made the political bosses at ease and gave them more freedom and confidence in dealing with the diamond mogul without feeling obligated to accommodate his views and comments in the policies of the government or the political parties except the unperturbed sailing of his business.

By the time when his influence spread broad and wide and his popularity soared higher and further, with the acronym JT acquiring a cult-like following in the Indian diamond bazaar, his ambition had to be diverted to the sphere of protecting his family lineage.

The news of the death of his only brother woke him up to the assertion he made to his father the day before he left for South Africa.

'I'm as determined as my forefathers were to bring laurels to you, my father, to my family, to my community, and to myself. And I will be at your and my family's disposal any time under any circumstances if any need arises,' he had said.

He had left the house of his father to seek fortune in a strange land with the promise to be useful to the family in times of need. When his father died, his brother was still there to be at the helm of the family affairs, shouldering the responsibility of protecting the family's name and the business it inherited—the business diversified many times in the past—to ensure the survival of the family's single lineage. By now, he had acquired wealth bulky and intense enough even to influence polity et al. in many African states, but he was childless and politely unhitched. His promise to his father was to be at the family's disposal if any need arose. His father would have condemned him to eternal sorrow if this time, when the demise of his brother, the anointed inheritor of the family lineage, was not regarded as the opportune time to be at the family's disposal. He had to protect and provide support to let the next generation survive and prosper and, most essentially, sustain the bloodline.

JT had done wonders in salvaging the businesses of his acquaintances and, most notably, that of his *liaison*, Irfan Rangoonwala. His intervention in the *Estrela* debacle was historic. His influence had significant weight, on a positive note, in politics of a few African countries, including Kenya and Mozambique. His image in the Indian diamond bazaar was that of a messiah.

So now, would his dispensation be enough to save his family lineage from extinction? His brother had left behind his wife who was so determined but was a novice in the trade, and his son, who was just a teenager and too young to display the inherited Baghdadi Jewish sentiment yet, a sentiment to sail through the most gnarled of business topographies.

JT could play a direct role by establishing active connection with the widow Hannah, providing personal support and protection to the inherited business, or else an indirect role by circumventing a direct faceoff with the widow and using a foster alliance in pretext.

Direct contact with widow Hannah was viable to re-establish the long-lost family connection and to cherish the family bond that had been missing since he left the house of his father. He would be a father figure to the teen Ezekiel and be a guide and protector to the widow as well as the business—*a bulwark never failing*. The widow would command more respect in the highly patriarchal society with a man behind her playing the role of a family patriarch. The business would be well fortified with endowments from his wealth—both money and knowledge.

Reflecting on the positive side, the benefits amassed huge temptation. But there was a rider. He had left the house of his family, promising only to be at standby in times of need. He had left the fate of his family business to the care of his brother. Running and prospering the business was not his duty any more but his brother's and, in his absence, the inheritor's. He could be of help in times of crises. He had left the house to build his own empire, primarily to avoid partitioning the family business and making survival in the extreme market condition more harrowing. This he did out of love for his family and his brother in particular.

With the theme of his leaving the house ricocheting in his mind, his consciousness permitted him playing only a limited role. He would play the role of an unseen godfather to the family until the boy attained manhood and could absorb the full responsibility of overseeing the business. He had faith in the boy that he would not run dry of wisdom and capacity to successfully run the business for he too was a lineal descendant of the adventurous Baghdadi Jews, who had a mindset polluted inherently with the hunger to succeed and outclass competitors.

The outcome of this decision to perform only a limited role in sustaining the family business was what made him choose Irfan Rangoonwala as his emissary to the widow Hannah and, more befittingly, as a liaison. In this way, he would redeem his pledge to his father and indulge himself in indirectly protecting the family. The most challenging thing would be not in extending support to the family in any form but in burying the guilt he would inherit in hiding his true identity for a long time, maybe forever. They were separate entities now, and he wanted to let it continue like that. He had gone his own way, building his own empire. Let his success not overshadow the unleashing of the true

CHAPTER 15

Diamonds mined from the open-pit mines near Gumira were mostly blue ones. If the mining had not been a clandestine one, the big stone discovered earlier by Emmanuel and co. would have made a terrible news with its size, clarity, and colour. It was an exceptionally vivid blue stone, a rare one. The precursors to this discovery of its same class of beauty were the ones discovered from the Cullinan mines near Pretoria in South Africa. Among these was the widely publicized and popularised stone dubbed Cullinan, which was discovered way back in 1905, a humongous 3,106-carat blue beauty.

Though the stone from Gumira was not a very large one compared to the Cullinan or the few large almost-flawless ones discovered in Cullinan mines later, it weighed roughly 420 carats, and its look displayed a class of its own. Even a layman's eye wouldn't miss the beauty and probably its value. This discovery was the main reason why Johann and his team of Rhodesians abandoned the mining activity to pursue their own lives beyond the clandestine world after reaping in abundance from the sale of the stone. If the stone had been mined legally and it been sold by auctioning in the open market, it would have fetched double, or much more, the amount they had disposed it for.

The stone was sold to a sheikh from the Emirates who wanted to cut it into three beautiful crystals representing his three beautiful wives. They would be embedded in the crowns and be on display in each of the three houses owned by his wives in his palatial compound. After his death, they would represent and be a soulful reminder to the visitors of his palace, his fine life, and the beautiful wives.

The discovery of a unique stone always seemed to act as a dampener to the illegal diamond trade. Instead of the players getting a boost to their morale and seeking for more discoveries and higher sales value, they preferred to make hay of the opportunity and quit the trade in toto. As in the case of Johann van der Watt and Emmanuel and friends, this too was the case when Peter Kabweza's people discovered a rare huge stone weighing about 380 carats in rough. So lovely was the stone and much adored by the militants that it was named Darling.

Darling was sold to a Russian businessman of Jewish descent who had a strong influence in the Duma and was also a good friend of Jonathan Tobi. The businessman had once served as the ambassador of the Union of Soviet Socialist Republic to Mexico during the vertex of the Cold War.

In the aftermath of the sale, all stakeholders—from the Mozambican military to Peter Kabweza—called it quits, which meant the natural acquittal of JT from the trade. The subsequent event led to Peter Kabweza's acceptance of a civilian role of his own volition before the election in 2005 and the amalgamation of his brigands to army regulars. The

Mozambican military, guided by a new defence minister, shed their aspirational role as harbinger of revolutions in the continent and drifted towards an internal role with more national commitments than following international agendum.

CHAPTER 16

For two whole months, the name Ezekiel Tobi dominated and probably illuminated the gossip circle of the Kathiawadi diamantaires, who could not easily recover from their shock and disbelief at how a family business, built and nurtured with care down the generations with successes in abundance and enormous market presence, could be dissipated within a fortnight by its legitimate and customary inheritor without any visible signs of stress or threat of insolvency to justify the act.

The Kathiawadis strongly revered the sanctity of heredity in a family business and of shouldering the responsibility of their fathers even if the inherited business was at a loss or almost in quandary. It was not about conquering new business avenues but propelling the inherited business to a new level of success or consolidation, depending on the health of the business, which always concerned them most. The sudden departure of the Tobi family from the diamond business could be like the legendary river Tapi disappearing suddenly one fine summer's night, leaving the city of Surat in a lurch for its goddess the next morning. It was simply an unthinkable situation. A few years ago, the success of the Tobi family had encouraged so many rumourmongers to come out with their illusory and spiteful allegations about their business dealings and linkages. Even the man who had espoused the theory of the existence of a Jewish triangular cartel ruefully eulogized the uneventful winding up of the Tobi family's stint in the diamond business as 'Diamonds are *not* forever.'

Ezekiel had kept with him the main building which had once housed the cutting and polishing section of their business, but not for any plan of restarting the business there in the near future. It was not essentially kept as a perennial source of income from the monthly rent it would generate either. It was spared the hammer to be a standing souvenir representing the once-thriving family business passed down the generations—though altered very few times before concentrating on diamonds three generations prior—but nixed at its prime.

The building would be from now on passed down to the Tobi family's newer generations again as the business it had once housed was passed down through generations before its unnatural death. It would represent the successes of the family in the bygone years and, most importantly, be a symbol that nothing was sacrosanct enough to last forever; even a business like the family's, which had once been at the height of towering success, was not immortal.

The building would stand the test of time and would represent the family's legacy for generations to come, but the most occupying thing for Ezekiel Tobi was what brought him to Adajan from their ancestral neighbourhood of Katargam. He had the option of disrespecting his oath to his dying mother and benevolently leading the charge to uplift the family business to a higher level of success.

But legend had it that the destruction of the Jewish elitist society in Baghdad was very unfortunately the result of the misadventures of some of the elitists in the community who were in cahoots with the invading Mongols in the AD 1260s against the wishes of the elders of the community and the rabbis. What they supposed would lead them to another era of Jewish prosperity had dragged them to decades of subservience.

This event served as a stark reminder to every Jew of Baghdadi ancestry of the potential hazard of egregious mistakes committed due to greed and ambitions against the wishes of the elders. The Baghdadi Jews who conquered all odds to settle down in the western coast of India had, too, come with a strong faith in this legend.

It was not only the urge to settle the riddle about the abbreviated initial JT his mother had drawn him into that led him sell off the business, but it was also the desire to discover the significance of the business term *liaison*, which was so unpopular but often spilled out inconspicuously by his mother, that attracted his intuition more.

If the secret behind the success of his mother's business endeavours lay in the coded term *liaison*, it was worth taking a plunge into the mystical pilgrimage to discover the truth beneath the layer of her success. The decision to hunt for the source of *liaison* was not his decision alone; it was a mutual thrust willingly supported by his wife, Bhumika Desai. The Gujarati women were well known for their emotional strength to let loose their husbands and for their enduring patience to wait for the overseas adventures of their spouses, who would make their return sometimes after as long as a year or five or ten but not without bringing home a bounty of wealth, or just to collect their wives to live together happily ever after in their newfound abode, with thriving businesses to cherish. It was a rare case for a husband to never return for his wife, abandoning her to the mercy of social subjugation. It was this trait of Gujarati women, the determined patience, that Bhumika Desai was displaying; she was no stranger to it, as every twentieth house in south Gujarat boasted of a relative settling abroad, whether in Africa or in America.

The first step for Ezekiel Tobi was to set out howsoever to meet Irfan Rangoonwala as his mother too had done when she was about to swear her allegiance to *liaison*. His mission now was different and was not for forging any business ties; he was on his way to discover the identity of the mysterious JT and, more importantly, the functioning of the alliance that they had so affectionately called *liaison*.

The Mumbai showroom of Irfan Rangoonwala at Dadar West was abuzz with crowds of customers—not an unusual scene, but much heavier than normal weekdays; buyers thronged the shop for the enticingly exciting festive offers going on for designer jewellery. Ezekiel proceeded towards the stairway, silently sidelining the bustling activities on the floor, and moved up to the stairway leading to the upper floor that housed the personal chamber of Irfan Rangoonwala.

'I appreciate you following the trail of your mother's business connections,' said Irfan Rangoonwala curtly, unfazed.

'It was her wish to discover who Mr JT is since she's missed the opportunity,' Ezekiel Tobi responded.

Irfan Rangoonwala said, 'She has immensely benefited from the generosity of Mr JT, and so it's obvious she would like to discover who he is.'

'That's what has brought me here—to fulfil her desires. And you are the first lead I can follow to discover this mysterious *philanthropist* who has been so kind to our family by propelling our business to such a high level of achievement. I am now duty-bound to convey my mom's special thanks to him in person,' said Ezekiel Tobi.

Irfan Rangoonwala replied, 'I don't think Mr JT would appreciate such a gesture, to be discovered just to receive your mother's appreciation. After all, *liaison* is good only for one generation. When your mother died, it stopped there. It died along with her, with all its mystery, and there is no inheritance as such. When I die, my business will be passed on to my son but without the benefit of inheriting *liaison*. He has to struggle hard to find another way out if he wants to run the business successfully. This 'one generation, one liaison' theory is strictly observed among the three of us, and it will die along with us. I know that is one thing that perplexes you, but it's in that secrecy where the beauty of *liaison* lies. So now, you have to look for another opportunity and not hunt down the mystery that has led your family to such a great height of success.'

Rangoonwala's unprovoked mention of the nuances of *liaison* enlightened Ezekiel more on the workings of the secret connection. It excited him more and encouraged him more so to discover its secrets and vices, though it sounded rather forbidden. He was surprised by the fact that *liaison* was such a mystery that his mother didn't dare to spell out its norms even on her dying bed though she explicitly requested him to discover who Mr JT was.

Ezekiel Tobi said pensively, swallowing his deep annoyance from Rangoonwala's outburst, 'I don't have any desire to discover the mystery behind your so-called *liaison* and have no interest in it either. I'm here following the trail to discover the man behind the alliance just to convey my family's thanks to him. Finding Mr JT will end my mission.

I will chart my own means of livelihood without your *liaison*, and I'm quite capable of doing that. It's more a mystery to us how a man so far away from India could be so generous as to propel our business to such a great height of success rather than your secret organization you affably call *liaison*.'

Irfan Rangoonwala said, 'As a matter of fact, hunting for the identity of Mr JT is the same as delving through the workings of the secret alliance. And I don't think I can be of further help to you. I don't want to be the source of the knowledge you are seeking for. You have your own liberty to go ahead but without taking my name along.'

The meeting ended abruptly there, without much headway for Ezekiel Tobi in prodding Irfan Rangoonwala further to extract better leads in his hunt for Mr JT. But this was partly in pretext; he was more interested in seeking the secrecy surrounding *liaison* than discovering its founder. He could understand the stubbornness of the members of *liaison*—or *liaisons*, as they referred among themselves—displayed at the slightest of provocation. His first experience was with his mother, and he found out now that Irfan Rangoonwala was no exception either. If this was the trend of the cult-like organization they were adoring, it would be quite imperative to note that the architect of this alliance would be no different and might be much harsher to deal with if confronted with the unsavoury request to open up *liaison*'s secrets.

Could it be that Irfan Rangoonwala wanted to be the sole beneficiary of Mr JT after his mother's death, and so he wanted to discourage him in finding Mr JT, which might probably lead to forging another tie or a separate liaison? Ezekiel Tobi felt Irfan Rangoonwala had lied about his real intentions. Irfan had also mentioned that his mother had been receiving major chunks of roughs from JT and that his own share was just a splinter in comparison. However, he had also said that he didn't feel that he was being betrayed or being used for a purpose because he was only still alive because of Mr JT, though he didn't mention the events that had led to his salvation.

Leaving the showroom with a feeling of dejection but with more abundant desperation to discover the myth about the secret alliance and the man behind it, Ezekiel Tobi promised to himself not to surrender to mere roadblocks like the one he faced today. It was rather a milestone. Every roadblock would spring up newer hints to his quest, a quest which bore the future of the family that had weathered through innumerable difficult situations dating back from the days in Mesopotamia to their arrival in the eastern shore of India while waltzing through the diktat of the Muslim rulers and the imposing trade conditions of the British Indian rule. His family couldn't be left defeated in a time when business conditions were most cordial and freedom and democracy were at their peaks. He would reinvent the family business at the completion of this holy pilgrimage. He would be revitalized by the spring of blessings he would attain at the end of the pilgrimage, a moksha of some sort for the enduring guidance for their business's resurrection.

He felt that the direction of his navigation—navigation for the path to moksha—had to be altered. If meeting Irfan Rangoonwala at Mumbai provided him not much succour to his mission, he had to restart the journey all the way from Surat again. He would delve deeper into the business formalities his mother had scripted so passionately. He believed the journey should start from there, and there were myriads of guides and directions hidden in the business formalities that the family had followed with rapt dedication from generations past.

His attention was drawn to the most important part of the family's business channel—the delivery system. The Tobi family, like all the other leading families in the diamond business, had also depended heavily on the age-old trustworthy services of the *angadias* as their sole means of correspondence and delivery.

CHAPTER 17

The angadias were the informal delivery boys, forming networks of delivery systems purely based on faith and consent. Their work could be likened to the unofficial banking-cum-courier service and is indeed very sensitive in the highly volatile diamond business. Their trustworthiness was proverbial and definitely out of the question; it had been handed down through the generations like an heirloom and sewn firmly into the texture of their culture as inseparable. Without the service of the angadias, the transactions in the diamond markets of Surat and Bombay (now Mumbai) would come to a complete halt. Such was the role of the angadias that faith in them also grew with their proven records of effectiveness and reliability with evolving time.

The other priceless quality they humbly possessed was their strange anonymity, which was an undeniable asset to those who sought their service. They were unknown entities to the world beyond their business circles. They were ordinary men travelling with ordinary citizens in ordinary trains and buses for ordinary work. In the age-old history of the angadias, there had never been an instant of a diamond heist being carried out with the involvement of the benevolent angadias; not even a cloud of doubt had been raised against their integrity. As humans, they too had their own shares of lapses in which diamond consignments had been misplaced or lost in transactions, but such incidents were hurriedly buried with the outright repayments to the senders for the value of the consignments—no argument or negotiation. They would pay up the money upfront.

Now the most vital link to Ezekiel's quest lay with the angadia firm they had employed over the years until he wound up the business. However, he understood that trying to extract information from the angadias would be no less daunting a job than that with Irfan Rangoonwala—possibly harder and harsher. He had to play another card, a plot more sublime and with a purpose devoid of any mischievous substance. There should be a marked difference with the straightforward approach and the clean mind he had employed in meeting Irfan Rangoonwala. And he couldn't be the businessman with a business mindset and an instinctively profit-oriented approach because that would entangle his confidence into defensive acts, which could be interpreted as a suspicious motive. If it went the business way, the angadia firm would not appreciate being kept out of the way and just being the source of information without getting any benefit in return and without any guarantee of their participation in the future. So it would be better to devise a means to seek a heart-to-heart meeting, like the date of young lovers, where the heart plays a central role.

This particular angadia firm had a reputation of secrecy and loyalty and had been the carrier and proud confidant of the biggest diamond families in Surat and Bombay, who were predominantly the offshoots of textile traders who had changed the course of their businesses' direction along with the movement of the compass of fortune of the time. These were the families who were adept enough to play second fiddle to the Jewish diamond barons controlling the world's biggest diamond trading centre in Antwerp until they mastered the trade from the Jews. They then overtook the controlling stakes in hoards in Antwerp City, like a midnight military coup, outnumbering and outsmarting the Jewish traders and significantly multiplying their profit margins to the point of being very undesirable to compete with by outsourcing the cutting and polishing activities to a destination with very lowly labour costs, their home state of Gujarat in India, which was out of bounds for the other trading communities, stonewalling them to the brink of bankruptcy.

This was until the Jews too started low-cost manufacturing from their home state of Israel in and around Tel Aviv City, but still it was very much a costlier destination compared to the labour costs in Gujarat. However, this made them significantly battle-fit, giving them higher margins to hold their breath for a moment at least. Behind the successful stories of the Gujarati diamond-trading families lay the angadias, who have faithfully couriered their inventories along the length and breadth of western India, particularly the Ahmedabad–Surat–Bombay belt. These angadias were basically deliverymen for textile trade between Bombay, Surat, and Ahmedabad. When the diamond trade began to grow and when many of the textile-trading families started shifting their business interests to the newly discovered sparkle, they used the skills they honed in the textile trade to deliver diamonds.

The owner of the angadia firm the Tobi family had had an age-long relationship with, Dhiraj Patel, was a third-generation angadia with roots in the Saurashtra region of Gujarat. He was a man who had been maintaining a low profile all his life in spite of the popularity of his agency among the very high-income traders. Definitely his service was out of bounds for the second- and third-rung diamond firms, who had to scout for the lesser-admired angadias. His trademark was his trustworthiness. There was a forbidden story proving his trustworthiness even in the most difficult time, which had never been relayed beyond the angadia circle—how he had married the daughter of a diamond trader who had been banking with them two generations prior but who went bankrupt due to the seizure of a large-scale consignment he had booked from the 'untouched' Western African source, the origin of the *bloodiest* diamonds.

The trader was doing exceptionally well with his solo exploitation of diamonds from Western Africa, which were smuggled by militants from the troubled Western African countries. He was said to have a rattling good relationship with Charles Taylor of Liberia, who had manipulative control over the blood diamond market of Western Africa behind the scene. The rendezvous point for the trade was Nigeria, the least suspicious country in Western Africa for diamond smuggling and whose export economy was dominated by petroleum products. Here Charles Taylor's men brought the ores and packed them for export to India, which were to be claimed by the trader at a predetermined location.

This trade was going well for a few years until the US intelligence agency, the CIA, penetrated the strata of Charles Taylor's loyal guards and later learned about the diamond smuggling routes of Charles Taylor. The consignment meant for the trader in particular was waylaid in South Africa, but without leaving behind any traces of being detected, it was set off again to its onward journey to India. The CIA followed the consignment with its men on board the ship replacing the original custodians. When the consignment was offloaded and sent to the predetermined location in Mumbai to be claimed by the trader, the CBI, an Indian intelligence agency was already tipped off by the CIA.

This was how the trader, who later on became the father-in-law of Dhiraj Patel, was apprehended by the long arm of the law. After being caught red-handed dealing in the illegal diamond trade, he was practically bankrupt. All his assets were frozen by the court at the initiation of criminal proceedings against him by the Enforcement Directorate, pinning him down from the angle of money laundering, a more serious offence than evading customs duties or other tax-related issues. The final judgment sentenced him to seven years of rigorous imprisonment. This was when the trustworthiness of Dhiraj Patel came into practicality.

When the incident occurred, Dhiraj Patel was already in his early thirties but was still a bachelor, already at a gloomily late age for marriage for a Gujarati boy. He was already the boss of the family business after his father suffered a massive heart attack two years ago, which left him incapable of handling the day-to-day business of their angadia firm. He had often rejected many an offer for the hands of their daughters by family friends and business partners, much to the annoyance of his father. His father confrontationally asked him if he was impotent after his fourth rejection and that too of a diamond baron whose daughter had just completed a fashion course from an elite fashion house in London.

Dhiraj's family and the family of the apprehended trader had the same family roots in a village near Rajkot in

Saurashtra. Their grandparents travelled down together to Surat to start an entrepreneurial life away from the burden of the stuttering monsoon-dependent agricultural life of Saurashtra. Their family bonds were of such a strength that even neighbours mistook them for real brothers. One started off with the business of recommissioning precious and semi-precious stones for jewellery, and another went for transporting textile goods between Ahmedabad, Surat, and Bombay.

By the time Dhiraj's grandfather shifted from textiles to carrying diamonds, the father of the apprehended trader also had moved on to real-time diamond business. The trader's father became the first patron of the sprouting angadia firm of Dhiraj's grandfather. The relationship grew even stronger when Dhiraj's father inherited the family business from his grandfather and when the trader too took up the helm of the family business, putting to the fore their brother-like upbringing to the advantage of their businesses.

When the trader was declared an offender to be imprisoned for seven years, Dhiraj came up with the idea of marrying the daughter of the tainted trader, much to the surprise and obvious chagrin of his family and to the utter disbelief of the trader's family, except for his father. He was even questioned privately by his mother about his real intention in marrying the daughter of the family so close to them but recently much ruined by their business practices. But he was steadfast in his decision.

His purpose was to insulate from the clutches of insecurity and fear the family which had sailed along his family in good and bad times since three generations back. His father understood his real intention and was never surprised unlike the others. Dhiraj had once told his father that trustworthiness in business was proven in the most trying times beyond the realm of business. These words resonated in the ears of his father, who thanked God for the birth of a true angadia who would carry forward the spirit of the faithful carrier beyond the influence of wealth and virtue.

Ezekiel had a difficult time getting an appointment with the much sought-after angadia who was colloquially called Dhirajbhai by acquaintances and competitors. He knew how his mother had formed a special professional relationship with Dhiraj, who had decisively defended any attempt to extract information regarding Hannah's source of raw materials, displaying his courageous angadia mentality, when prodded by many of the diamond traders at the height of the allegation about a Jewish triangular cartel and other baseless accusations that followed. He was enlightened enough to know that since many of those diamond traders were his patrons, he could lose chunks of his business, but defending the privacy of his client was his priority even if that might end with a losing streak also. He boldly declared that he would have done the same for any of his other clients if prodded for their source and delivery destinations as a true angadia man with no blemishes on the ethic they preserved and professed since his grandfather's years.

But in truth, it was a long-due repayment to the Tobis for the favour they'd shown Dhiraj's grandfather and his fledgling firm when he was hunting for loyal patrons to carry forward his angadia business venture. Ezekiel's grandfather had reposed faith in the ambitious Saurashtrian and contracted him for all his delivery requirements and later on banked with him for all his payments as well as receipts. He was the second person to employ the services of Dhiraj's grandfather and the first to utilize the banking option when their credibility was still doubted in the market. This relationship was carried forward remarkably unhindered by Ezekiel's mother, Hannah, when she took up the responsibility of running the family business after her husband's death.

Dhirajbhai, as a professional angadia, did a major chunk of supervision himself, attaching great deal of importance to the safety and security of the goods and the patrons his firm was dealing with. However, a pretty considerable time to spare for the son of his ex-client—yes, even a once-priceless patron—with no business interest attached was something he personally disdained; his trustworthiness would be tested when it was beyond the business realm. That was why it took him a week's time to accept the Ezekiel's request for a personal tête-à-tête.

Ezekiel Tobi said, 'You have shown remarkable perseverance in protecting the interests of my mother's business when she was at the storm of alleged shoddy dealings.'

Dhiraj said, 'The allegations were baseless and were just to demotivate her business sentiment. I knew well how the dominant males displayed their intolerance and ego when a businesswoman encroached upon their dominion with such a velocity of success. I was the one who couriered most of the goods, raw or polished, so I knew very well there was nothing much that was unusual to stir up such a storm of controversies except for their grudges against her business growth.'

Ezekiel said, 'I too am convinced that my mother was a fearful businesswoman who could defend her interests amidst intolerance for her success, but in reality, all her successes were not scripted by her alone, as you too are well aware of. By saying "nothing much that was unusual", you meant something unusual was there. Meagre as it might be, there was something unusual behind her business success.'

Dhiraj replied, 'Yes, something unusual was there but not vastly as the others'. Every one of those who enquired about her dealings knew the allegations were not as high profile as they themselves were involved in, but just to give your mother a harrowing time, they put together their intolerances. Your mother was one of the few diamantaires who could turn few opportunities to their advantage. Her business acumen was of the highest degree. And in the meantime, she could show the greatest concern and understanding to her business associates, including me. She never meddled with their affairs or encroached upon their interests. Only few of the biggest diamantaires whose businesses are still intact and in good shape till today showed this trait, which helped them in the long run and survive the stiff competition. They are the few people who understood profit-making cannot be an all-out self-aggrandizing affair to survive in the long run.'

'My mother had only two confidants in her business— you and me. You were her confidant even before I came to the picture. So you and I can't deny the involvement of a third hand, a powerful one, in her business process. Whatever the degree might have been, it was significant,' Ezekiel spoke matter-of-factly.

'If that is the reason you approached me today, I'm afraid I can't be of much help to you. If you say you and I can't deny the existence of a third force in your mother's trading activities, let it be. Why do you want to approach me just to confirm your knowledge?' Dhiraj said with an expression of annoyance.

Ezekiel replied, 'It's not my mother alone who has chosen to repose faith in dealing with your angadia firm. My grandfather had chosen your grandfather's fledgling firm, which had no proven market record that time, to deliver his precious goods, which could have endangered his business if there were any occurrences of theft or robbery. He trusted in a man whom he saw as possessing a quality of a true businessman, and more than just trust, he accorded faith in him by calling him a bankable man. You will remember that my family was the first to accept your grandfather's banking option.

'Our family was thankful to our faithful carrier of many years to whom we could rely on in totality with no fear of disloyalty. My father had no hesitation in continuing to utilize the services rendered by your family. Since my father died young, my mother took up the position of running the family business, and she too never repented in utilizing the services of your firm. But after her death, the family's business has to be disbanded—I'm sure it's not permanent—for the betterment of the future generations so as not to taint the family's legacy with failures. Without the participation of the third force, as you called it, the family's business would have headed for doomsday sooner.'

Dhiraj was aptly attentive this time, a feeling of guilt boiling up in his blood for displaying such an arrogant and unreasonable attitude towards the family that had been kind enough to trust them even before anyone else did. If this was not the time he could pay tribute to the souls of their most loyal patrons, when would the time ever come?

'If you think we are not worthy any more of your audience, I do apologize for the inconvenience. Indeed, we are reduced to rubbles and have no value to your interests any more.' Miffed, Ezekiel stood up from the chair and was set to leave.

'I am so sorry, Ezekiel. I showed my arrogance at the most inappropriate time. My family had always felt indebted to the patronage we had received from your family for years. Please, I'm sorry, I shouldn't have talked the way I did.' Dhiraj erupted in apology.

The hours that followed were spent in a free, fair, and frank discussion on how much they both understood Hannah's style of doing business, her ores that were routed from the source in a horseshoe-shaped manner from one point of contact to another to deflect any chances of detection, and most of all, the person from whom she sourced the ores.

Dhiraj said, 'When your mother approached me with a proposal to carry ores for her from Mumbai and that too with a pickup point so unfamiliar and unknown in the diamond business circle, I was suspicious of her intention. But however unfamiliar the pickup point was, the man who traded these ores to India was more of a mystery. And I was compelled to meet him, without the knowledge of your mother, to prove my trustworthiness and loyalty. Though it sounded weird to meet the man to prove myself, my worth, and my credential, it was a rare chance which I treasured later on. I met a man with so much dignity and authority and who, I later on came to understand, had a span of influence so overwhelming that he can get you out of trouble or entangle you with troubles that could gobble up your fortune. The meeting itself was a culmination of his deepest concerns for your family's well-being. It was arranged by his right-hand man in Mumbai, a dreaded underworld don to whom I have close affinity with.

'He told me that of all his business ventures, this was the most important one for him, to which his soul was attached to. It was not the value of the business but the legacy it carried along that was so important, which I failed to understand till now. He told me if I couldn't observe silence and secrecy, it would be wise to withdraw myself now so that another faithful carrier could be recruited.

'It was then that I decided to prove my worth and show my capability. That decision had opened up so many new things for me as well. I took the risk in trusting the mysterious man, and in turn, the mysterious man never failed to reward me abundantly, though behind the back of your mother. Let me confess that the one who had exerted the strongest influence to lessen my father-in-law's punishment was this man. His influence ran deep even in the judiciary. You may not believe it though.'

Ezekiel said, 'So defending my mother's interest was merely the culmination of the relationship you had built with the mysterious man and not out of respect or loyalty to my mother.'

Dhiraj clarified, 'That's a mistaken perception. The mysterious man, whose name I understood as just the initials JT, was all in favour of your mother's well-being. He would do anything for that matter, even to the extent of favouring me. I stood by your mother, and JT stood by me when I needed him the most. I may confess that I can't and won't have any direct dealings with JT. I was there for the sake of your mother. And business with your family was not a recent happening. It had gone through the generations, and so it was my rightful duty to defend your mother even if JT had not appeared in the scene.'

Ezekiel told Dhiraj, 'Before she died, my mother left me with her one delusional wish to be fulfilled at any cost.

She could have asked me to continue our family's business, carrying on the momentum that had been built over the years. However, she was in favour of me finding and meeting the man who was the source of so much blessings for us instead of blindly continuing with our business. She wanted me to resume my role as the heir of the Tobi lineage only after I could ascertain who this mysterious man was.

'And I would request you, as we had always been the receiver of your favour, to help me in contacting and meeting JT. Your family won't mind showing favour to the great souls of my mother, my father, and my grandfather, who had always been very partial towards your family when showing favours.'

Three days later, Dhiraj came to Ezekiel's house in Adajan; he was empty-handed but had a mind potently loaded with a highly sensitive idea, a hare-brained idea at first glance. His soul was never at peace since the day Ezekiel left his chamber after asking for a favour, descending on him a poignant reminder of the journey both their families had undertaken together but now withered. His life would have to endure a soulless journey henceforth, he regretfully believed, if he could not be of help to the Tobi family at this crucial juncture. His adage 'Trustworthiness in business is proven in the most trying times beyond the realm of business', which had shown him the way to courage throughout these years even to the adoption of his choice of a life partner in a most uncommon way, came back to haunt him at this time, vengefully giving him moral qualms in avoiding the plea.

A month after the meeting, after concrete analysis and research, Ezekiel left again for Mumbai now armed with the detailed layout of a highly explosive plan. If everything went well, he would set sail for a destination in Africa in a month's time. If the plan didn't work, it was simply deadly— suicidal to be precise. But there was no better a way out at the moment, and an alternative might be non-existent. They knew with a certainty that Mr JT lived in Nairobi. It was not a matter of landing down in Nairobi and going to knock on his door for a friendly chat like you would do to get better acquainted with a newly arrived occupant in your neighbourhood. Ezekiel needed a key to enter the gate to meet him, a notional key not for physical possession but akin to the key to the gate of heaven given to the Son.

The plan was, in brief, to kidnap the ruling don of Mumbai underworld, Vincent D'Souza, to hold him for ransom. The bait—jealousy.

CHAPTER 18

In the colonies of lowly houses in the northern fringe of Juhu Beach bordering Versova and surrounded by high-rise apartments like impregnable forts of medieval era was a house facing the seafront, looking strikingly ancient with its decaying wall paints and dark-tanned terracotta tiles adorning the roof. The look of the house was whimsically odd even when comparing it with other houses in the colonies. While other houses were bedecked with common colours—like white, blue, or yellow on the walls and green, blue, or black on the doors and windows—this house was painted orange all over. The oddness was more intense when you discovered the lone inhabitant of the house.

The lone inhabitant was Anitha Farreiro, who was of unknown descent; many mistook her to be Goan but having stronger links with Pondicherry in South India. She was the only child of the late Mr and Mrs Ravi Farreiro, who were in the business of biscuit-baking till their unfortunate end in the infamous Lockerbie bombing on their first overseas travel. The year was 1988. Anitha was seventeen then. She was attending a junior college in Pune reputed for mentoring students for future entrances in elite engineering and medical colleges.

Anitha came back to the house alone to take charge of the situation. The next day, she flew to London with a representative of the state government to visit the site of the crash as the closest family member of two of the victims aboard the fateful plane and to collect a few remnants of the ill-fated plane in order to perform a symbolic funeral back home.

Upon landing back home, she was accorded a stately welcome at Bombay's international airport, with the state government announcing and handing over a compensation of 200,000 rupees on the spot as the only daughter and only child of Mr and Mrs Ravi Farreiro, two of the victims of the bombing from the state of Maharashtra.

Anitha didn't return to the junior college. She didn't continue with the family's business either. She lived on the compensation from the state government and, later on, a much larger sum received from the flight operator Pan Am as next of kin of the victims.

One misty December morning, five years after the Lockerbie bombing, she locked the house and handed the keys over to the next-door aunty for caretaking until she returned; she promised to pay an allowance for the favour in addition to the 100 rupees paid in advance. She didn't come back even after a year. That was the time when she was rumoured to have married a merchant navy officer from Goa. A reliable source from the locality admitted the marriage as fact, having heard it from the nephew of the bridegroom who attended the ceremony at a beach in North Goa. However, three years later, the girl returned to the house, bearing no sign of a married woman—no rings on her fingers and toes, no *mangalsutra*, no bangles as usual, and incidentally, no man accompanying her home either.

There ended the first part of the uninteresting life story of Anitha Farreiro. In a year, all the rumours and gossips peacefully died down altogether like the smokes of a candle blown out by a breeze from the window and vanishing peacefully into thin air.

The second part started another four years later with the sighting of an unusual figure in the locality. The man was a strange figure in the locality but was well known to their eyes for their sighting of him in televisions and print media in connection with many unpopular events in the city. His name commanded dread. The usual sighting time was when darkness descended overwhelmingly in the evening and neon streetlights of the insufficiently lighted streets were the only source of light in the area. You could say that would be after 8 p.m. and that too only on Saturdays.

The veranda of Anitha Farreiro was always lighted green but dimly on Saturday evenings from the first sighting of the man in the locality. On other evenings of the week, the veranda was always spotted with a bright white light.

The love affair of Anitha Farreiro and Vincent D'Souza was spontaneous. And it was a case of *love at second sight*. The first time they met, both agreed there were no unusual chemical and biological reactions boiling up in them, as they confessed later on. The second time they met, accidentally and unexpectedly, it was love that followed them all the way.

Their first meeting was at a reception of a common friend's wedding. Vincent D'Souza seldom came out openly in public functions due to his unmistakable stature in the underworld—not for fear of being apprehended by the police, but to avoid causing uneasiness among the people at the functions. The only public function he had previously attended after going underground was the wedding reception of his only niece, where he vehemently forbade payment of any kind of dowry. He disdained marriages solemnized with the spirit of greed. He told the boy's family that if they wanted any dowry or help of any kind, they could approach him twenty-four hours a day, seven days a week. His presence at the function was a testimony to his strong standpoint. Never ever did the boy's family demand dowry from the girl; rather, they treated her royally ever after.

He attended his friend's wedding reception out of respect for his unconditional help during the tumultuous time of the stock scam. This was the man who had saved his life and helped him escape and move underground. In the reception, Anitha and Vincent met for the first time in their lives, being introduced by their common friend. It was just a hi–bye situation. Some pleasantries were exchanged, but nothing productive happened. Both of them soon swayed away to their own circles without carrying any special effect from the meeting.

The second meeting was just the opposite of the first, and it was quite eventful as well. Vincent D'Souza was on his way to the personal office of a builder, a flamboyant one, who had a howling success in the construction business under his protection and was a regular payer of tithe to him. His entry into the office was welcomed by an unusual shrieking sound of a woman's voice emanating from the personal cabin of the builder. He opened the cabin door and was surprised to see Anitha Farreiro wailing disparagingly at the builder. There was a pin-drop silence momentarily.

'Anitha Farreiro!' exclaimed Vincent D'Souza, and looking at the builder, he enquired, 'She is my friend. What's wrong tonight?'

Anitha Farreiro stormed, 'This is the third time he cut on my commission from a buyer.'

At that moment, there was a visible nervousness pouring out from the face of the builder. He knew if Vincent understood the real issue, he would be most unhappy. Vincent D'Souza, though a don of a great underworld family, always stood for fair deals in business and had always been supportive of the weaker gender on their plights. Most of all, Anitha Farreiro was his friend.

'There are some small pending issues with the buyers, and that's all. There are no payment issues with Anitha,' the builder said, hiding his nervousness as much as possible.

'So you deducted her commissions because of your issues with the buyers,' said Vincent D'Souza coolly.

'There were no issues at all even with the buyers. He is exploiting the vulnerable ones, boasting of some kind of protection he enjoys from the underworld,' exploded Anitha Farreiro again, without knowing the other man in the room was an underworld don.

The builder had no more strength to justify his misdeeds. He knew his fate was hanging by the most slender of threads, ready to snap at any time since Vincent D'Souza looked remarkably unhappy due to him taking unwarranted deductions from someone's rightful commissions and taking wrongful advantage of his protection. He took out a chequebook from his drawer, filled up a page, signed on it, and handed it over to Anitha. The amount was handsome, much more than the sum of the thrice-deducted commissions, about four times more. He profusely pleaded for their understanding. Vincent didn't utter a word. Both Vincent D'Souza and Anitha Farreiro left the scene together unapologetically.

Vincent took Anitha to one of his palatial hideouts on the city's outskirts. With no personal tête-à-tête or no personal enticement, both of them entered the elegant bedroom unrestrained and enjoyed the wildest and most satisfying sex both had ever had. That was a Saturday night.

The next morning at dawn, Vincent disguised himself as a taxi driver and dropped Anitha at her house in the colonies of lowly houses in Juhu. After a while, Anitha dressed herself up in a bluish kurta and left for the church not far away from her house for the Sunday morning mass. It was the first time she attended the morning mass in two years. She attended the mass for a thanksgiving or repentance, she was not sure. However, there was a sparkle in her eyes, undeniably displaying a sign of satisfaction in life.

Ever since then, Saturday nights saw almost-regular encounters of the two lovers at the Farreiro house. Nothing changed even after years of their celebrated relationship and their sexual intimacy except for the venue; not once did they go back to the hideout again for sex. The Farreiro house was the permanent spot. Every Sunday morning after Saturday night's encounter, Anitha Farreiro would always sport a colourful kurta and attend the church for a mass for reasons not known even to her.

It was a Saturday evening in Juhu. The summer sun unwillingly descended from the skies above the seas, lighting the nimbus clouds like halogen lights tenderly illuminating the Rashtrapati Bhavan on the night of India's Republic Day. As usual, at the corner on the seafront, a house so distinguishingly coloured from others displayed a unique light on the veranda again. Could the green light be a sign of welcome to the visiting don? Or else, could it be a warning sign to the locals to stay away from the vicinity since a great don would be visiting? These were the questions that had been baffling the people of the colonies for years, but they were never brave enough to intrude any further, fearing to invite the anger of the ruling don. And never did words spread out from the locality about the unusual event that descended on them on most Saturdays.

Vincent D'Souza entered the house, most nonchalantly crossing himself at the crucifix hanging opposite the entrance door. His paramour looked as charming as ever. Dinner was ready and laid out, and beyond that, a happier moment was awaiting them. The dinner tonight was special, as it was the anniversary of their first tryst on a Saturday night a few summers ago, and this time, it did fall on a Saturday. The dinner was sumptuous, and their intimacy was evocatively more passionate than other Saturday nights barring the first. They had hardly finished their dinner before both of them tumbled down to the nearby sofa, vigorously embracing each other as if trying to re-enact their first sexual encounter. The ensuing lovemaking was proudly sensational, their endurance level unwittingly remarkable and athletic.

The next morning, an hour before the first rooster crowed, Vincent left the house discreetly, fearing to evoke the senses of the neighbourhood at odd hours. A few hours later, Anitha too was on her way to the church for the Sunday morning mass.

On her way back home from the church, Anitha heard a benevolent-sounding voice calling her name from behind, 'Anitha Farreiro.' She turned back and saw a young man with a gentlemanly look following her from a short distance and waving at her. The man looked unfamiliar, but his good appearance convinced her to wait for him. He was not so tall, and he had a lean build, looking similar to those of

Anglo-Indian descendants still possessing more European than Indian features, with whitish skin colour and blue eyes.

'I'm Ezekiel Tobi,' the man introduced himself.

'Do I know you?'

'You don't, but I have known you through a study of your family lineage.'

'That's interesting. But what have you to do with my family tree? And who are you?'

'That's an explanation I can give you if you can spare me some more time.'

Anitha took the man to her house. Ezekiel pulled out a copy of the Torah from his bag, putting it on his lap while sitting on the handsomely designed cane chair and looking at the confused lady. He introduced himself as a Jewish man from Surat who had profound interest in preserving the old traditions of the Jews in India who, though they migrated from different parts of the world a few hundred years ago, were bonded by a common cultural heritage.

'I am here seeking the revival of our old traditions and searching for evangelists for the safekeeping of our dying traditions,' he declared imperatively.

'But I'm not a Jew,' responded Anitha.

'That was what I too would have believed if I had met you earlier or befriended you before I studied the history of some of the oldest families of the Jewish people in India who had immigrated to different regions of India from different parts of the world,' replied Ezekiel, then added, 'You would find it hard to believe that your great-great-grandfather was a scholastic man who was well-versed with the Torah. He even taught for a while at a synagogue in Cochin before retiring back to Pondicherry. He was the son of a Turkish Jewish trader who came along with the French force and married a French lady in Pondicherry.'

Anitha's look changed from confused to curious. She said, 'No one has spoken to me about our Jewish connection before, not even my parents.'

Ezekiel continued his narration, 'It was from your great-grandfather that the Jewish link was severed altogether when he married the daughter of a French missionary and professed Catholicism. He became more of a Frenchman than a Jew. He abhorred Jewish tradition, though he could still follow the tradition by being a Catholic.'

Ezekiel Tobi explained to Anitha Farreiro about his mission and his inclination to educate the children of the descendants of the new age's 'lost tribe'. He wanted to enlighten them on the wisdom buried in the Torah and the rich culture of the Jews, though it should not be construed as an attempt to win them over to the religion of Judaism, which he himself did not profess any more.

He said, 'You can be a Jew by being a Catholic, a Protestant, or a Hindu. It is a tradition and an identity which we need to keep alive.'

He told her that he decided to dedicate two months a year for ten years to a person belonging to the Jewish ancestry to teach her or him the Torah and other Hebrew literature. He would also fund a pilgrimage to Jerusalem after the two-month teaching to visit the Temple Mount, where the controversial Dome of the Rock stood, though the exact purpose of the visit would be unknown since it was forbidden by orthodox Jewish rabbis due to the *holiness* of the site; the Dome of the Rock was very sacred to the Muslims but was more deeply sacred to the orthodox Jews, who regarded the mount as the site where Solomon's ancient temple once stood, akin to the claim of the Sangh Parivaar on the site of Babri Masjid in Ayodhya, which they reverently regarded as the birthplace of Lord Ram.

This selfless dedication of a man so concerned about the conservation of his ancestral tradition deeply impressed Anitha. She was influenced more because of her newfound ancestry. Without much thinking over it, she decided to be the first person to take up the two-month tuition. The tuition would be three times a week on alternate days, starting from Monday, and would be in the evening when routine works of the day were done.

The first week appeared to pass through fruitfully and peacefully, but not without drawing the notice of Vincent D'Souza. Saturday night came. Everything was in order as usual—the desolate street leading to the Farreiro house, the green light, and the aroma of a finely cooked dinner emanating from the house. However, Vincent's manner of entry to the house tonight was unprecedented. He neglected the crucifix for the first time and did not cross himself, and he failed to notice the beautiful look of his paramour standing near the kitchen door. He moved straight to the dining table, and possessing a sombre look, he demanded of his paramour who the hell had visited her for three nights this week and without his knowledge. Anitha had never seen Vincent looking so perturbed and serious as tonight. She wanted to laugh her heart out at the jealousy he displayed for the first time in their years of courtship.

'He is my teacher. He is teaching me the tenets of the Jewish Torah and basic Hebrew for a deeper understanding of the ancient Hebrew literature,' Anitha promptly declared with an innocent smile on her face.

'So what's this newfound interest in Judaism all of a sudden?' said Vincent sarcastically.

Anitha replied with a simmering annoyance descending on her face, 'I have the least interest in Judaism. I'm a practising Catholic, if you want me to make myself clear. But as a Jew, I'm interested in knowing and learning our great traditions and culture to benefit the future generations.'

'Oh God! What soul would interpret your bleak and unrecorded ancestry and link it back to the Jews if not to take advantage of your gullible nature? It's all to win your heart for some personal gains.'

Anitha Farreiro felt hurt by the careless remark about her ancestry, but she swallowed her anger so as not to prompt the argument into a fight. It gave her more determination to continue the study of her very own culture and language and the beautiful traditions it inherited.

Anita felt that the dinner was tasteless, with the continuing soulless remarks about her new enthusiasm by none other than her own soul mate. The lovemaking afterwards was dismal and artless. The night was stupidly long to her dismay. She had never felt this way in the years of their relationship.

The next morning, after Vincent D'Souza left the house like a *highwayman*, she was still lying on the bed, all too awake from the night and undetermined about what she would do next. She didn't get up to kiss him goodbye, nor did she get up just to bolt the door after he left. This was her first defiant act in their relationship. She left the door unbolted, and it didn't bother her in the least. And she did miss the Sunday morning mass as well.

The tuition continued for the second week. Anitha found it more interesting than before and found herself more attached towards her tutor. The dullness she endured during the first week due to the strangeness of the language which could have been her mother tongue otherwise had only vaguely lingered on. She felt strongly and wishfully that it would disappear on the third week.

The last teaching day of the week ended peacefully again. Saturday night came, and it would have been deeply troubling had this incident happened two weeks before or more. Anitha was the least interested in the upcoming event and felt disturbed at how to receive her partner of many years since their relationship became strained a week ago. She tried her hand in cooking a delicious South Indian dish and lit a green light on her veranda but reluctantly unlike other Saturday nights. However, she heard no sound of footsteps on the corridor or twisting of the doorknob even after 10 p.m. Even till midnight, she sensed no sign of the don's arrival. Prior to this, on the few Saturday nights he missed, Vincent always announced it beforehand, at least a day or two. Instead of feeling hurt, Anitha felt emancipated. She had lost interest in the man who had no respect for her feelings, she believed.

The third week was more cheerful. Anitha felt liberated from the stranglehold of a chain that had cuffed her from freely pursuing her newfound interest. Even her progress in Hebrew was visibly good. She was determined to get the best out of the man in two months and pursue by herself the study of Hebrew and its literature after that. What she also found out was that she felt comfortably peaceful in the company of her tutor. She felt secure and admired in earnest the enthusiasm of the man so selfless in his approach and so dedicated in his mission.

And the Saturday night of that week looked different altogether. Anitha developed a different approach this time, mentally and practically. First of all, there was no green light in the veranda, and secondly, there was no burning desire for meeting the man whom she used to love more than anything else. She didn't expect him to turn up this time after their minor scuffle and the dispassionate sex two

Saturdays back, so there was no hectic time on cooking as well for a special guest.

However, Vincent D'Souza arrived unannounced. He barged into the house like a hurricane and moved in like a commando storming a terrorist hideout; he caught the neck of a dumbstruck Anitha standing near the kitchen door as if to strangulate her. Among his many demands for explanation and the one he disliked the most was the strange timing of the tuition—i.e. night-time—when there was plenty of time after sunrise in the morning till sunset. He confessed to have understood Anitha's new desire for learning the language and culture of her newly discovered roots but would not tolerate any longer the odd timing of the tuition. Anitha remained silent and looked obstinate, displaying a behaviour of being the least bothered by Vincent's demand.

'You will see his head hanging on your front door next Saturday night if the timing is not rescheduled by next week,' Vincent D'Souza announced the fatwa and left the house.

Unlike other nights, the atmosphere during the tuition of the next Monday was distressing and unpleasant and most inappropriate for teaching and learning. Anitha looked tormented and sounded like she was hallucinating. She narrated the likely consequences of continuing the tuition at night and, more categorically, the capability of Vincent D'Souza to do what he had said.

'He is the ruling underworld don of Mumbai,' she said and paused.

Ezekiel Tobi, sounding concern and care, suggested a way out from the threat. He proposed the tuition to be shifted for a month at his residence in Surat and to let her trauma calm down under his wife's care, which he said she needed most at this time. Meanwhile, it would let things settle down; hopefully, Vincent would make amends for his behaviour. Anitha was humbled by the good gesture.

The next morning, Anitha Farreiro was seen leaving her house with a man carrying a suitcase for her.

CHAPTER 19

Vincent D'Souza was furious, and he fumed with anger and hatred, knowing how the duo had escaped his diktat by moving to Surat. His personal ego soared higher and higher to a level he had never tasted before. He would not be at peace until he showed his capability to the man who dared to take away his girl from his purview; his threat to the girl of hanging the man's head at her door was not just a cruel joke. In depth, he felt his virility was being mocked at and subjugated to another man's mercy. This hurt him the most. This gave him a sleepless night.

The next day, at early morning, he left for Surat with a .22-bore revolver tucked in a holster underneath his leather jacket. All this he did at the height of his burning ego and without any clear motive or mindset. He did not take any of his closest men into his confidence either. He felt his manhood, not his power, was at stake. Meanwhile, he failed to notice even with his inborn feline instinct that he was being watched. From the time Ezekiel and Anitha left for

Surat, Mumbai's vital stations had been manned by Dhiraj's wide network of men, the angadias. They kept watchful eyes on the foolhardy man who would follow the urge of his jealousy to the extent of risking his life. When Vincent boarded a train in Mumbai Central, wearing a leather jacket in a summer morning, it was all too palpable and clear that he was armed. Dhiraj was instantly briefed about the development.

Dhiraj had readied two sets of arrangements for two possible contingencies—armed Vincent and unarmed Vincent. Since Vincent came possibly armed with a weapon, he had to be disarmed before his entry into the city and entrapped without any mishap like a wildcat blindly chasing a bait into a trap.

The train slowly chugged into Surat Station and halted when the engine reached the northern end of the platform, aligning exactly with its length. Then everyone was taken by surprise—and even more so, Vincent D'Souza—at the railway police personnel standing ready near the doors of every compartment, frisking passengers alighting from the train. This was the first time in years that passengers were being frisked and checked at the station very elaborately. The last time was when an anti-Sikh riot was feared to spread from Delhi in the aftermath of the assassination of Prime Minister Indira Gandhi. Dhiraj had given credible intelligence to the police about a man armed with a pistol, travelling on a train to commit a political murder in Surat. Seeing the frisking at the doors and the doors on the other side being watched by police personnel from the opposite platform, Vincent had no other option but to leave behind his pistol in the toilet.

The police didn't seize any weapon after frisking the passengers at the exit doors. But just when all passengers were checked and the police were about to abandon the scene, the ACP ordered the checking of all the rooms and toilets in the train for a final round-up. That was when a revolver with live rounds was found in the sink of the toilet of an AC coach. The carrier of the weapon had sneaked past the police along with the other passengers, leaving behind his weapon in the toilet.

Outside the station, Vincent D'Souza was mobbed at the gate by autorickshaw drivers, not an uncommon scene outside the station, asking him his destination and promising to drop him off at the best hotel in town with the most competitive rates. All these drivers were Dhiraj's men. The real rickshaw drivers had been shooed away for the day, tipped off with a few hundred bucks. Among them, Vincent thought the elderly looking bearded man would know best where he wanted to go as the place where the Jews lived in the city would sound secluded and unfamiliar to most young people. Actually, there was no such place any more, where the Jews settled in a colony in the city. He knew that the man who took away his girl was a Jew, and he believed, with his untrained knowledge in the history of the city, that the Jews were still living in Surat.

Vincent asked the elderly man if he knew of a synagogue in Surat or somewhere Jewish people lived in the city, explaining to him what a synagogue was and who the Jewish people were with simple analogues. The man gave him a positive nod and told him the place would be none other than Rustampura.

The riskshaw driver drove him towards the old walled city area of Rustampura. If the driver were to be believed and if Vincent's historical knowledge of the city were a tad sharper, the likely destination would have been on the other side of the city in the opposite direction of

Rustampura—Katargam, where there still existed a Jewish cemetery and where the Jews had settled once upon a time. Rustampura did not in any way fit the description given by Vincent D'Souza. It was the most unlikely location if you look at the history of the Jews' settlement in Surat. But Vincent D'Souza, without the appropriate knowledge, was convinced and driven there by the driver.

Rustampura was perhaps like a mini fortress, an independently distinct locality within a city in the depth of the old city's inner circle, connected by various congested lanes and by-lanes from different directions but isolated from the life and time of the city itself. Its narrow roads were as confusing as footpaths diverging in a wooded forest, not revealing the destination just by a peek through but being chosen purely by faith. If you were a first-timer sneaking into the middle of this mini fortress, you would likely be entangled in the cobbled streets, desperately searching for exit points for minutes until you unshackled yourself to see the light of the city on the other side with the help of one of the good inhabitants. This was a place where even a postman with five years' experience in the area sometimes ended up in dead ends while trying to leave the place after making a few deliveries.

In one of these suffocating, congested streets surrounded by walls of old dwellings with small windows, Vincent and his driver were approaching the other end when another autorickshaw was seen approaching them from the opposite direction. There was no space for bypassing in this narrow street even for small vehicles like autorickshaws. Meanwhile, another rickshaw appeared at the back, blocking the way even for a reversal to make way for the approaching rickshaw from the opposite direction. Vincent didn't sense any danger yet.

Two men from the passenger seats and the driver of the approaching auto got down and walked towards them. The same scene appeared behind. This was when Vincent D'Souza felt strangely unnerved and woke up to reality—this was not his fiefdom here. He was in danger, possibly fatal, he sensed.

One of the approaching men shouted, 'Vincentbhai, we are not going to hurt you if you cooperate with us. We need to interrogate you for some basic clues—that's all. You will be set free, and you can continue your *hafta* collection in Mumbai.'

The voice of the man sounded satirical. Vincent knew his capacity was being mocked at, especially with the mention of hafta. He was wrong to believe that only his manhood was at stake when he left for Surat; his dictatorial power was also thrown into uncertainty due to his stupidity in venturing out far away from his controlled-area all alone. He realized this more and more within a fraction of a second, and he felt a scary shudder go through the length and breadth of his spinal cord.

He was unarmed, and there were no possible escape routes; they were surrounded by a thick lining of walls dotted with a few highly placed small windows and doors. He had to surrender. Surrendering was the most disgusting act a man could ever do; he had felt this very recently. He once had said to his compatriot, 'The cowards surrender, the fools die unnatural deaths, but the brave always live or die for a cause.'

He felt even before he made an official surrender that he had surrendered himself. There was no other way out. He would be subjugated to their will. His inner anger grew more with the feeling that he was going to be humiliated. A man folding so many protectees under his wings was now in someone's custody and mercy. If his protectees knew about this, his humiliation would hit the heavens. He preferred to be killed than to let the world know about his present condition.

Two men from behind reached for his arms and handcuffed him. He didn't make the slightest of struggles. His didn't utter a word. His emotion drew him closer to Jesus and his sufferings at the hands of his captors.

Jesus had suffered silently, and so will I, his mind resounded. Isaiah had prophesized 700 years before Jesus's birth, 'He was oppressed, and he was afflicted, yet he opened not his mouth; like a lamb that is led to the slaughter, and like a sheep that before its shearers is silent, so he opened not his mouth.' It was like the prophecy had reoccurred about 2,000 years after Jesus's crucifixion or about 2,700 years after Isaiah's. He correlated the two events. He was humbled.

This was the first time he remembered the sufferings of Jesus Christ since he went underground after the stock scam that savagely rocked the Indian financial market about a decade ago. He couldn't recollect the last time he observed Lent. He repented it.

One of the captors, who had the longest beard, knocked at the door on the western wall about five yards from his position, one of the only three doors Vincent could see in the long and high-walled enclosure. A man with a white robe opened the door and exchanged a few greetings with the bearded man. The man did not look perturb nor paid attention to the captive; he seemed satisfied with just a slight glance at the captive. Vincent was let into the house and deep into another room, crossing three more doors inside, he counted.

Who on earth will be able to detect my captivity? he wondered and was numbed by the enormity of the helplessness surrounding him.

He was seated in the middle of the room, on an iron chair inelegantly cushioned with a jute-braid cover. At this time, he couldn't imitate his saviour, Jesus, any longer. He shouted, 'Why am I being held captive? I need to know the reason immediately.'

None of the captors seemed mindful to his demand. They were the least bothered by the echoing of his voice in the thick enclosure, which was like the voice of a caged king of the jungle—so dreadful in the jungle but incapable of evoking terror if caged. A voice—not from the men in the room, but oozing out from the four corners of the room—responded.

'Vincent D'Souza, you are not under our captivity. You are our guest here, and you will be with us just for a few days,' the voice from the corners said. 'You are in a cabin surrounded by speakers and microphones. Any time you need to talk to us, go ahead and speak. We will respond to you immediately.'

'Why did you take me to this enclosure then?'

'We will let you know when the appropriate time comes.'

'Then who are you?'

'You will not know about us even after you are given farewell from here as our guest. But we assure you that we are not your enemies.'

'How long am I going to be here?'

'For that matter, I will connect you to a PCO in Dharavi. Speak to the owner, one of your trusted lieutenants, and tell him that you are in Surat, safe and happy. Tell him you will be back in three weeks. If not, your followers might dissipate, with their leader being untraceable. We don't want to ruin your business.'

Vincent was connected to the PCO, and he told the owner exactly what he was told to say. Nothing more. He felt, however, that his dignity was completely eradicated. His situation now was not better than that of a circus animal following the instructions of the owner.

The voice was heard again from the walls, 'Thank you, Vincentbhai. Rest for the day. We will talk again tomorrow to discuss real business. The handcuffs will be removed soon. For food and drinks, you will be provided the best in town.'

A brief beeping sound was heard after the voice, and an echo of silence followed—pin-drop silence.

The next day, almost at noon, the same voice from the previous day echoed out in the room again. Vincent looked at his watch. If it were Mumbai, he would have dozed off at this time round for his regular siesta. But today he was as awake as the bats were at night.

'Today's session will be frank and blunt, Mr Vincent D'Souza. And we are going to discuss real business,' the voice said bluntly.

Vincent was silent.

'Mr D'Souza, would you mind making another call today? But this time, not to your lieutenant, but your mentor.'

'What nonsense are you talking about? Who do you think is my mentor?'

'We want you to talk to your mentor in Nairobi on our behalf.'

Vincent remained silent for a while. A gloomy, pale thought descended on him like the sudden arrival of high waves on the shore, and he experienced a nervousness he had rarely experienced before. If Mr JT knew he was under someone's captivity, he would do anything to free him, he knew.

However, it would be of extreme humiliation for me, he told himself. Instead of letting Mr JT know about his captivity, he wanted to let him find his body somewhere and learn about his kidnapping after his soul had left his body. That would be more liberating than letting him bail him out from this situation and surviving with his tail between his legs.

'I'm not going to call him even if you torture me to death.'

'We are here not to torture you, Mr D'Souza. We just wanted you to talk to him normally, just a courtesy call.'

'Why can't you yourself make the call and talk to him?'

'We want you to have a simple chat with your mentor. Nothing more than that. And in three weeks' time, you will be on your way to your beloved Mumbai.'

'I don't think I need to make a call to him in your presence. I have my own set of protocols in talking to him, not under your guidance.'

'Let me be frank. As I said earlier, we want you to make a call to him. If you don't, we are not going to do any harm to you anyway but to Anitha Farreiro. We know where she is.'

Vincent realized that he trembled for the first time in his role as an underworld don—not out of fear, but out of love. He came to realize how much he loved Anitha. Though he had thought she underestimated his capacity and manhood, actually it was his love for her that drove him out of his secure zone. He could even let his captors chop off his head for his defiance, but could he let them do any harm to Anitha due to his own folly? She was in grave danger just because of him, his blind jealousy and foolishness included.

'You can do whatever you want to my body, any kind of harm, but please leave Anitha alone. She doesn't have to pay the price of my foolishness.'

'Mr D'Souza, we don't want to do any harm to you as I have said. We will let you survive so that you can continue your profitable hafta collection in Mumbai. You are so important there. But we think Anitha has no worth there. She has to be eliminated.'

Vincent was deeply enraged at the comment. His role as a great don had been mocked at here. He felt that they were not treating him with more dignity than a caged parrot, which could be released at the will of the owner. And he was angered more by his incapability to protect Anitha at the moment. His once-dominant power in Mumbai was just a vanity in Surat. If anything was left of his prestige, it wasn't even worth the ego of a concubine.

'I will talk to him,' said Vincent with self-hatred and submissiveness. He understood that if his flock of followers heard about these words, words of utter cowardice, they would desert him in haste. He was ashamed of what had become of him.

A dial tone of a phone echoing from the walls followed.

'Hello!' the voice from the other side said.

Vincent understood he had been directly connected to JT's house. 'I'm Vincent D'Souza,' he said.

The man on the other side identified himself. He was JT's trusted man and his housekeeper. Both of them exchanged some pleasantries. After a while, JT picked up the phone.

Both of them had hardly enquired about their well-being when Vincent was disconnected. He knew the line was deliberately disconnected, and he felt elated at not talking to JT in great length with discomfort and guilt. But he didn't know that the call was taken over by the man behind the whole scheme.

'This is Ezekiel Tobi,' the man frankly introduced himself.

'What do you want?' came the reply from JT.

'Your man Vincent D'Souza is in our custody. We don't want to do any harm to him, please know that.'

'Then why is he in your custody?'

'Give me an appointment to meet you at Nairobi. After that, he will be released safely. No further demand or negotiation.'

'Done. Come and meet me any time,' said JT, and the phone went dead.

Ezekiel was puzzled by the easy acceptance of his condition. Could there be any sinister attempt behind this? He was content with the fact that whatever JT might be planning, they held his man in captivity for a barter in the worst-case scenario. He would leave for Nairobi tomorrow; permission was at hand now.

Meanwhile, Anitha would be sent to Jerusalem for a pilgrimage as part of the promise for taking up the Hebrew class. If everything went well, by the time Ezekiel landed back in India, she too would be back from her trip. This timing was essential for further dealing with Vincent D'Souza and for keeping Anitha engaged during the hauling up of her lover without her knowledge.

The next morning, Ezekiel and Anitha were dropped off at Mumbai Airport by his good friend Dhiraj for their onward journey to Dubai. Ezekiel promised to accompany Anitha till Dubai to help her catch another airliner for her onward journey to Tel Aviv. This was a good alibi in the pretext of goodwill to hide the real intention of his travel— to fly to Nairobi from Dubai.

CHAPTER 20

Ezekiel was received at the gate of the estate of Mr JT by a well-dressed black gentleman of great height and elegance and displaying a calm and philosophic look. The man introduced himself as Richard, the caretaker of the estate. The house he saw at not so far a distance from the gate was not as large as he had expected it to be, but it was built provocatively beautiful in design; the design was either Korean or Japanese, he couldn't determine immediately. But it was abundantly oriental in looks.

There could be four to five bedrooms, he analyzed at the sight, *not extravagantly large for a diamond baron of such a stature.* The vastness of the compound was overwhelming, dwarfing everything that existed in it—the trees, the flowers, the ponds, and the guardhouses. And that could be the reason why he found the house rather smaller than he had expected it, the vastness of the expanse fooling his vision.

They entered the house from the main door, which opened directly to the main hall with a walkway on the right side proceeding to a splendidly set kitchen. The hall or the main living room was beautifully decked with unique-looking furniture and art collections; the art collections implied the vastness of cultures and civilizations that had flourished and were still flourishing around the four corners of the world, including menhirs from the Aztec kingdoms of the past, a plaster-of-Paris sculpture of a pregnant Bavarian lady, a wooden kangaroo with a beer bottle crafted by an unknown Australian farmer, a stolen copper Shiva Nataraja from sixteenth century Thanjavur in South India, and an original spear of the first pontifical Swiss guard of the Vatican City. The walls were elegantly decorated with two vast paintings hanging on opposite walls and facing each other like two beautiful contestants in a beauty pageant confronting a judge to decide who was more beautiful of the two.

Can't be Van Gogh's, Ezekiel observed, *but aren't very inferior.*

On the middle table was a glass vase beautifully adorned with flowers he had never seen before; they were pinkish in colour and down-facing. His eyes always had admiration for flowers and could identify most of the common species of flowers at one go, be it of the roses or the lilies. He could tell the flowers in the vase were of the lilies, but their colours and forms were strikingly unfamiliar. He was slightly touching the petal of the flower in admiration when a voice from behind brought him back to his senses.

'The Dzuko lily,' said the voice from behind. 'Among the rarest of the rare wild lilies.'

He turned back and saw Richard standing behind him, staring at him and displaying a warm smile.

162

'I have never heard of that name before, Richard.'

'Mr JT has a weakness for lilies. And he did some craziest things to collect and grow the rarest lilies in the world. We have successfully grown five of the rarest species of lily here.'

'That is the least I expected to hear about him.'

'You may not believe how much pain we had to undertake to flower those lilies here in Nairobi,' said Richard. 'That particular lily, the Dzuko, is native to northeast India and can grow only in a particularly small patch of hills in a sub-Himalayan region, an area large enough for three football fields on the high and treacherous but beautiful Dzuko Valley on the border of Manipur and Nagaland states.'

'That sounds interesting.'

'I was among a three-member team sent by Mr JT to collect the soil from that mountain valley to grow the flower here. The journey to the valley was four hours on foot from the nearest town. Imagine how many coolies we had to hire to carry the soil to the town named Mao and have it transported by Maruti Gypsies to Imphal Airport and then airlifted by Mr JT's private jet. I didn't even mention the trouble of getting permission from the Manipur state government for collecting the rare soil.'

'You collected the soil, and so you grew the lily here successfully?'

'Growing the lily here was the most difficult part.'

'How did you accomplish it then?'

'Mr JT hired a well-known professor in botany from Princeton University with a reputation of well-acclaimed research in the flower species. The professor consumed almost two years in research before we tried growing the lily here in Nairobi under controlled conditions in a greenhouse. He took several months studying the records and researches on the plant in universities in Manipur and then camping himself at Dzuko Valley for about a year to study the soil, the weather patterns, the seasons, the environment, etc.'

'Was it not a madness to spend so much money on something like growing lilies?'

'You may say so, but it has also earned us wild praises from the most powerful offices in the world. There is this particular incident which I am proud to tell everyone who comes here for the lilies. It was the wedding of the daughter of the prime minister of Kenya, who happened to be a very good friend of Mr JT. Mr JT promised the girl that her wedding bouquet would be an ensemble of the rarest and most beautiful of lilies in the world. The wedding was attended by high dignitaries from across the world, including the first lady of the United States. The first lady was so distracted by the beautiful bouquet that she enquired of the bride about the flowers. The bride referred her to Mr JT. Mr JT, following his own stimulating style of speech, eloquently narrated to the first lady about the five species of lily that adorned the bouquet. I could see the first lady was deeply impressed and morbidly influenced. But I found Mr JT rather mean when he concluded with a provocative, though blithely said, punchline: "The White House won't be able to sacrifice a sizeable budget to grow the flowers in Washington DC.' Ha ha . . . We also presented her with the book *The Five Lilies*, written by the Princeton botanist on his research wholly and wilfully funded by Mr JT.'

'Amazing!' exclaimed Ezekiel.

'And then Richard named this estate The Five Lilies without consulting anyone, not even me,' interrupted JT on a light note, entering the hall from the door, and the three men ended in a light laughter.

'Ezekiel Tobi, the son of Hannah, the lady with a heart as hard as the diamond she dealt with. I am here to listen to what you want to say,' Mr JT continued cordially after the short spell of laughter.

Meanwhile, Richard slipped off to the corner on his way to the kitchen, giving the duo liberty to carry on an unrestrained conversation.

Ezekiel replied, 'Coming here and seeing you already conveyed half of what I wanted to say.'

'What is the other half then?' demanded Mr JT.

'Thank you,' said Ezekiel. 'That was what my mother wanted me to convey to you personally. I have achieved what I have promised my dying mother to deliver come what may.'

'Is that all?'

'That's all. But it has caused me a fortune to earn the right to say so.'

'You need not thank me for anything. It was the fulfilment of the promise I too had made to my father, as you did to your mother.'

'What promise had you made to your father?'

'My father, who was your grandfather.'

'What did you say?'

'Yes, your grandfather. I'm your paternal uncle.'

'I knew my father had an elder brother who had left the house of the family to seek fortune in a foreign land, but the family never heard of him again. He was rumoured to have died in South Africa at the peak of the apartheid regime.'

'His name was Jonathan Tobi, and I'm here right in front of you, still alive and still dreaming big. JT for Jonathan Tobi.'

'If you are the real Jonathan Tobi, what made you stay away from the family for so long? You didn't send words of condolences to my grandfather and my father when they died.'

'Condolences were not my promise. To stand by the family when needed most was what I told my father I would fulfil even at the cost of my life. And I did that. So you are here today to find me.'

This revelation from the diamond baron controlling a vast network of businesses today from diamonds to oil now hit Ezekiel hard, hitting him as if to wreck his nerves out of his senses. Was he daydreaming? Was he confronted with a lie that had good chance to be linked up with his long-lost uncle?

He was damned, he thought, damned because he need not hear such a testimony from the baron, whether truth or lie. He was there just to convey the thank you from his mother. This made him at a loss for words, unable to utter what was in his mind.

The short spell of silence was broken by the voice that had just wreaked havoc in the mind of Ezekiel. 'I knew you would one day find me, even just to fill the thirst in your blood. That trait you inherited from our ancestors. That day, I had decided, would be the day I will hand over the running of my business to you, my son, Ezekiel Tobi.'

Ezekiel was still speechless and was surrounded by an aroma sprinkled with anger and joy—anger at his newfound uncle for not bothering to contact his family throughout those years even at the death of his grandfather and his father, and joy of finding the long-lost family member long believed to have died in foreign shores and the joy of fulfilling the last wish of his mother.

Ezekiel retorted back, 'You have gone your own way to build your empire, forgetting your family. I am also capable of building my own empire but by taking my family along.

I don't need your hard-earned wealth to lead my future life. Keep them to yourself. I'm going my own way.'

'I'm not forgetting my family in any manner. I kept a promise to be with the family in times of need. I did that. You should appreciate my way. I left the house to give way for your father to inherit the family business. I love my family more than anything else. That was what your mother reaped, though unknowingly.'

Hearing of Mr JT's sacrifice to let his father inherit the family business slowly eroded his anger, letting him rethink his approach towards his uncle's offer. He knew it was true, and it was true indeed. The family's business was handed down to the next son since the death of Hosea Tobi to his grandfather. There was confusion in the family with the birth of two sons, he had learned. However, until today, he knew not of his uncle's sacrifice to survive the family's unwritten law of inheritance. He had shown his reluctance, so he did not want to give in without another struggle.

'But I am not taking over your business. I am going to build my own empire from scratch now that I have fulfilled my promise to my mother.'

'I have kept the business for you, my son. I haven't married to keep alive the family tradition of inheriting the business to the lone descendant. You are my only descendant. You take it, or you break the family tradition.'

'You're going too far if you let your business be handled by a new entrant. The oil business, your refineries in Mombasa, and the crude-oil imports and refined-oil exports—they are too complicated to handle. Give them to experts, or make a board to handle the conglomerate. I will be your assistant, maybe from Surat or from here.'

'I will be assisting you for the rest of my days,' said Mr JT assertively.

And that was all that was required to end the formality of handing over the reign of the empire to a new blood.

Then Surat was emptied of the last remaining Baghdadi Jews, though *polluted* with another bloodline in the last days of their sojourn. Another chapter would be opened in another continent across the Arabian Sea, which their forebears had crossed from the opposite direction to conquer a new business avenue in India. The flow of the wind, the wind of fortune, had reverted from west–east to east–west. Only time would tell if the family tradition would survive the advent of capitalism and technology bundled together as faces of the same coin, requiring the best of brains, not family values, to outperform peers in the market.

EPILOGUE
Surat, India

Anitha Farreiro came back to Surat from her pilgrimage to Jerusalem, embracing more abundantly her newfound identity. She would go back to her home in Juhu to lead a refreshed life, a life so enlivened by the discovery of her ancestral roots and its beautiful identity and marvellous culture in a world so wholesomely bothered by wealth creation and hunger for power than traditional values and ethics.

Ezekiel Tobi came back from Nairobi with a satisfaction and success he had not envisioned to be possible when he first set out on foot to hunt for his mother's benefactor and fulfil her last wish. Had he tried struggling on his own in a highly competitive diamond market without the backing of a godfather, his days would have been numbered, and he probably would have withered. He obediently undertook the pilgrimage his mother had set him on, and that had made all the difference.

Vincent D'Souza was released by his captors near Surat Railway Station, with his eyes tightly covered with a bandana and with a ticket to Mumbai tucked in his pocket. He would never know who his captors were. He didn't want to know them either. He learned the fragility of life the hard way. Even the strongest man could kneel down and surrender his dignity for the sake of freedom, freedom not necessarily for himself but for his loved ones. Life was valuable when you appreciated your partner's choice of happiness. Vincent would not demean Anitha Farreiro's newfound happiness in the culture of her ancestors, provided she would accept him again as her partner in her remaining life's journey.

Printed in the United States
By Bookmasters